NOT REALLY MARRIED

BARBARA MCMAHON

Chapter One

Keith Branson pulled into the driveway and stopped behind Drea's car. Slowly he cut the engine and got out. It was twilight, that soft time between day and night when everything was still and the light faded slowly. The old house was dark. He could hear the crickets as they began their nightly song.

She had to be home since her car was here.

Slowly he mounted the shallow steps to the wide wooden porch. He wore faded, worn jeans, a dark blue cotton shirt opened at the throat, rolled up sleeves, and scuffed running shoes.

His expression wavered between bitterness and anger and grim determination. The past year had been unbearable.

He'd lost everything. Lost his wife, his business, his home.

For a moment, painful memories stabbed and hot anger surged through him. He controlled it, clamped down tightly as he had since he'd first discovered his wife's betrayal.

Reaching the front door, he peered through the long oval glass in its center. No glimmer of light showed in the recesses of the house.

He rang the bell.

A minute later he rang again.

Blast it all, she had to be home. Where would she go without her car?

Yesterday at the funeral she'd looked so alone.

That's when he had his first glimmer of the idea. He'd thought of nothing else since. Becky had insisted he come by to check on her. He'd taken it as a sign.

So he'd come.

And now he'd propose the crazy scheme to Drea. He couldn't imagine her reaction, but he hoped she'd agree. If he could be persuasive enough. With Drea Stephen's help, he'd be able to pull himself out of the financial morass he'd found himself in and get his life back on track.

He hated depending on anyone—especially a woman. But the opportunity was too good to let slip by.

And it'd only be a temporary dependency. Just long enough to solve his money problems.

If she'd agree to the terms, that is.

Walking around to the backyard, he spotted her. She sat alone on the wooden swing that hung from the overhang of the big back porch. Alone in the dark.

He skirted one of the many islands of flowers in the sea of green grass and waited for her to notice him. The dahlias and snapdragons and petunias were full of vibrant colors during the sunny part of the day. Now in the waning light they were an indistinguishable gray. Only their fragrances lingered in the air like a haunting melody. He smelled the honeysuckle that clung to her back fence. The sweet scent reminiscent of the flowers at yesterday's funeral.

She'd looked so alone at the grave site. So lost.

"Andrea?"

She looked up. "Keith? What are you doing here?"

Taking the brick stairs to the big back porch, he crossed over to the swing and sat beside her.

She'd been crying. He could see it on her face and in the soggy tissues she clutched in her hands.

The sundress was rumpled, her feet bare. For a second something twisted deep within him.

"I came to see how you're doing," he said softly.

Without thinking, he reached out and drew her up against him, his arm comforting around her shoulders, his chest something solid for her to lean on.

She relaxed against him and gazed out over the dark yard.

He'd known her for years. She'd been his younger sister Becky's best friend since high school. She was almost like a sister to him.

Though he remembered suddenly what a crush she'd had on him when she first met him.

He smiled without humor. He hadn't thought about that in years. She'd outgrown that crush ages ago. He now hoped the tie between their families was strong enough to lend support to his crazy idea.

"How're you doing?" His voice was low, soothing.

"I'm okay. Just sad," she said softly. "I'll miss him so much."

"I know. I'm sorry."

Her father was the last of her family. Her mother had died long before they'd moved to Norfolk when she was sixteen.

"I saw you yesterday at the funeral. Thanks for coming," she said softly.

He slowly rubbed his fingers against her upper arm, trying to think of something to say that'd comfort.

Trying to think how to bring up the subject uppermost in his mind without sounding crass and insensitive.

"What are you going to do now?" he asked finally.

Drea shrugged. "Go on, I guess."

"Did your dad leave you the house?"

"Yes. It's paid for. And I have my job at the library."

"Becky said you'd sold a book. I thought maybe you'd quit the library to write."

"Only one book's been published so far. I'm glad Daddy got to see it. But I don't get any money until after the royalty period's over. And then how much will depend on how well it sells. There won't be anything left from his insurance after I pay for the final medical expenses and the funeral. I still need my job."

"Plan to be a full-time author one day?" he asked, watching the sky darken to night. The crickets seemed to rev up, their buzz louder as the night grew darker.

It was still hot and humid. It probably wouldn't cool off before morning when the sunrise assured another hot day in the Tidewater.

"I'd like to, but it'll take a while. I need to support myself in the meantime. I'm almost finished with line edits on a second book and will get back to it soon. Just not right now."

The last piece. This was the last piece to make the plan work. It had to. It'd benefit them both.

"Drea, I have an idea I want you to consider," he began hesitantly.

Suddenly he realized how much he wanted her to say yes. He needed to present it properly, to make sure he gave her no reason to refuse. He had to show her how it'd benefit them both.

"What?" There was a thread of interest.

"I guess you heard about Diane and me from Becky?"

The bitterness was sharp. The anger surged fresh and hot again, though the discovery of his wife's betrayal was over a year old.

"I was sorry to hear you were getting a divorce," she said slowly.

"It's final. Was a couple of weeks ago. Did you also hear I'm flat broke, haven't anything to my name but my clothes?"

He tried to keep the bitterness from his tone.

Drea sat up at that and tried to see him in the darkness.

"No! Keith, what happened?"

"Diane went through everything we owned, the savings, the investments. Ran up huge charges on our credit cards before she took off with her lover. It cost me everything to pay the debts. I had to sell the house and liquidate the business."

For a second the rage threatened to flash out of control. He'd been so stupid, so blind not to see that his wife's compulsive gambling was ruining her, them. By the time he recognized what was going on, it'd been too late.

"You had to sell your business?" Drea said, disbelieving.

"Had to liquidate everything to meet the final settlement.

After all that, I still owe five thousand dollars. And without the heavy equipment, all the tools and no credit to speak of, I can't operate. There're too many other construction firms out there to compete with. I lost it all."

"Oh, Keith, I don't know what to say."

She reached out and touched his hand.

"How about your dad? He'd love for you to go back into his business with him."

"No. At least not now. I need to prove to him and to myself that I can make it on my own. Besides, one reason I went out on my own to begin with was because his ideas are too old-fashioned for me. We were constantly clashing."

He pushed the swing slowly, hoping he could present his plan in a way so she'd accept.

"I may have a way to recoup. But I need some help. Your help if you'll give it to me."

"Of course, you know I'm happy to help however I can. But what can I do? I don't have much money. All we had went for Daddy's last medical expenses."

"I don't need your money. I need you. I've been offered a job with Markham International."

"Working for someone else? Oh, you'd hate that. At least working for your father you know one day the business would be yours one day."

"I told you why I can't work for my Dad—at least not now. Markham's huge, worldwide in fact. Their bid for a job in Kuwait was just accepted. They're paying top dollar, with bonuses, housing and a living allowance."

"Even so-"

"It's the perfect chance to earn fast money. I figure I can save every penny beyond bare-bone living expenses, most of which will be furnished by the company. If I go, it'll be for three years. At the rate they're paying, I'll have enough to start over when the assignment's finished. More than enough."

"Then it sounds as if you should go."

"Yeah, I think so, too. There's only one hitch. Because of some problems in Kuwait with rambunctious servicemen, Markham's taking no chances with an international incident. They're only offering jobs to married men if their wives go with them."

"Oh no." She was silent for a long moment, then peeked at him again. "Is there any hope between you and Diane?"

"Not a hope in the world. If I never see her again it'll be too soon for me! But I need a wife."

He hesitated. He never thought he'd ask the question again. "Will you marry me, Drea? Listen, before you say anything. We would not really be married except on paper. I'll support you entirely. You wouldn't have to do anything but live in the same house with me. It'd be purely platonic. I wouldn't expect marital rights or anything like that. The way I feel about women now, I never want to get entangled again. But I need this job and the only way to get it is to go over with a wife."

"Marry you?" Drea looked astonished.

"In exchange, you could write full-time. Not have any financial worries while you build that writing career. You could rent this house, quit your job at the library. By the time we return, you'll have had time to write several books. You'll be well established as an author. We'll get a quiet annulment and go our separate ways. I'd give you whatever help you'd need getting established again. What do you say, Drea? Will you help me out? We'd be married, but not really married."

He knew from Becky that Drea didn't have a special male friend. She'd rarely dated this last year with her father so ill. There was nothing to tie her to Norfolk. And he hoped he made the offer enticing enough that she'd accept. She'd just said she'd like to write full time. Here was her chance.

The silence was heavy. Even the crickets stopped their ceaseless symphony. The stars in the sky sparkled in the velvet night, the wafting scent of honeysuckle filled the dark stillness. Time seemed to stand still as he waited for her answer.

"Okay, Keith, I'll marry you."

Chapter Two

One year later

The drone of the airplane should have been soothing, but instead it kept Drea awake. She gazed out into the inky darkness. Even if it'd been bright daylight, there was nothing to see but the clouds covering the Atlantic. It didn't matter. She stared out into the endless night, wishing she could hold time still.

Everything happened so fast. She'd known all along it would end one day. But she hadn't expected the end to come so soon, so abruptly.

She glanced at Keith, asleep beside her. He looked so infinitely dear. His lashes were dark and thick, curling against his cheeks, such a contrast to his sun-bleached blond hair. The lines beside his mouth were relaxed in sleep, not slashing deep as when he was awake and in tight control.

She turned back to the window, her thoughts chaotic. Over and over the droning of the plane hummed the refrain: *it's over, it's over.*

She'd agreed to be his wife for the three-year tour in Kuwait. Yet their time had been cut short by two years.

Was this how Cinderella felt when the clock chimed midnight? Disbelieving, denying, desperate?

She longed to turn back time, to start over again. She wished she still had their future spread out before her.

Instead, suddenly and unexpectedly, it was ending due to his father's heart attack.

She gripped her hands together. It'd only been two days since they'd learned of Keith's father's attack and the fact that open-heart surgery was his only chance of long-term survival. When Keith asked for emergency leave from Markham, the company had granted it immediately. They were returning to the United States, the assignment in Kuwait behind them. Drea didn't believe they'd return; there'd be too much for Keith to do at home.

And so the need for their marriage was over.

Tears slowly slid down her cheeks. She brushed them away furtively. She'd agreed to the terms. She'd known when she accepted that it came with an ending date.

He wouldn't understand tears. He wouldn't understand how she ached with the thought of the annulment that they'd discussed casually at the beginning.

And she hadn't fully realized how deeply she loved him. Or how much she'd ache each day living with him and keeping that love hidden.

She hadn't expected to hurt this much. A distant future had been easier to handle before knowing their lives together were over and she'd be alone for the rest of her life.

"Drea?" Keith drew her hands from her face and turned her slightly. "What's wrong?"

She shook her head. "Nothing." She quickly brushed away the last of the tears. "Just thinking about things."

"Honey, you need to get some sleep. It'll be a long time before we're home. We have customs in New York to get through, and then a three-hour wait for the flight to Norfolk. Come here."

He reclined her seat, pushed up the armrest that separated them and pulled her against his side, tucking her head beneath his chin. Lightly he brushed his fingertips across her cheek, drying the last trace of tears. He held her gently, as a brother might, settling back in his seat.

"Are you worried about my dad?" he asked softly.

She nodded.

Let him think the tears were for others. She leaned into his comfort. His hold on her reminded her of the night after her father's funeral. Keith had held her then and it'd been wonderful. That'd been the night he'd asked her to marry him.

From the time she'd first met him at age sixteen, she'd loved Keith Branson. In the beginning she'd been open with her adoration, but the teasing she'd received taught her to hide that love and to let it go.

He'd never thought of her as more than almost a sister.

She hid her pain when he married Diane, hard as it'd been. His marriage hadn't dimmed her longing to be with him. She always listened avidly whenever Becky spoke of her brother, wanting to learn all she could about every detail of his life, even though he'd long ago moved beyond her reach.

Slowly the steady beat of his heart soothed her. Slowly the strain of the past few days caught up and she began to relax into sleep. She'd hidden her love all these years. Nothing had really changed.

Feeling her soften against him, Keith shifted slightly to get more comfortable, wondering why she'd been crying. He hadn't seen her cry since her father's funeral. Since the night he'd proposed. What caused her tears tonight?

Fear for his father? Maybe. She'd known him a long time. As a teenager she'd always been in and out of their house, almost as at home at his folks' place as Becky.

Was she remembering her own father and his final illness?

She should be delighted they were heading Stateside. Happy as a clam that they'd left the desert and all those restrictions behind them. He knew he was glad to be going home. He'd saved every dime he could to repay the last of the debts. Once they were paid, he'd begun to build savings from which he could operate when he returned home. He could have used the additional income from two more years of work, but he knew his father needed him—at least until he was back on his feet.

It'd be good to be back in single-family-home construction. The heavy construction work in Kuwait was not his forte. The money was good, but the work almost mindless and definitely boring.

And the restrictions in the country had been stifling.

Yet he'd put up with it all to reach his goal—to get free of debt, to rebuild.

How had Drea viewed it he wondered for the first time.

She never complained. She kept their apartment spotless. Her cooking was even better than his mom's. And she'd always seemed so cheerful, no matter how many hardships they'd experienced, like the time the water was off for three days. She'd never once complained. When the power went off with great regularity, she only commented on how hot it got without air-conditioning, but never uttered a word beyond that.

He couldn't have chosen a better partner to live with this past year. Diane never would have survived, even in the early days when he'd thought everything was going well in his marriage.

He'd been smart to ask Drea. He owed her.

When Keith opened his eyes, dawn glimmered through the plane's windows. Drea was staring out across the gradually lightening sky. Had she slept for long?

"Are you all right now?" he asked.

She turned back and regarded him with solemn brown eyes. Nodding, she remained silent.

"We should be landing soon," he said, checking his watch.

"It's been a very hectic couple of days," she said, watching him, taking in every delectable inch of the man. From his light sun-streaked hair worn a trifle long, to the wide expanse of his muscular shoulders, to the long legs sprawled out as much as the seat in front permitted, he personified masculine perfection.

She sighed softly, her heart swelling with love for her husband. Her husband in name only.

Sadly she turned to look back out the window. Living with him the past year had been a tightrope walk between delight and despair.

She loved him so much she could scarcely contain it.

Yet she knew he saw her as no more than a kind of foster sister. Someone to help him out of the financial bind his first wife caused.

She'd been very careful to act consistent with the way he saw her, though every instinct urged her to throw herself into his arms and tell him how much she loved him.

"I didn't get a chance to call the Realtor and ask him to give notice to the tenants. I'll have to do that as soon as we arrive in Norfolk," she murmured absently.

Already the tasks ahead seemed to stack up.

"There's no rush."

"Where am I supposed to stay when I get back to Virginia?"

He stared at her for a long moment. "With me," he said slowly. "Where else would you stay?"

"Our agreement was to stay married for the time in Kuwait. You don't need a wife in the States. You made your position very clear before we married. Check that prenuptial agreement if you've forgotten," she said tightly.

That'd been a sore point with her. He'd had an attorney draft up a legal document that would have made a saint angry. She understood it. He was still raw from Diane's actions. But it'd pierced like a sharp piece of iron.

If she let herself think about it, she'd get angry all over again.

"Well, for heaven's sake, we don't have to separate the day we reach the States. Good grief, Drea, you can't think I'd turn you out the minute we land. You're like a sister to me. We get on fine. What's the rush?"

"No rush. I'm just trying to live up to our agreement. It was for Kuwait only, right?"

He frowned . "I know our marriage was for Kuwait, but another few weeks or months won't change anything. We thought we'd be there for three years. Let's not rush into separating. I don't want my dad to worry about anything until we know he's going to get well."

"You're the one who doesn't want to be married. After Diane, I thought you swore off women forever."

"Yeah, well, that was a while ago. And I earned enough money to start up again on a limited basis. I couldn't have done that without you, honey."

His fingers brushed against her cheek.

"It was a mutually beneficial agreement, if you'll recall. I couldn't have written as much as I did if I'd still been at the library," she replied fairly.

"Two books in less than a year's pretty good. And just think, once we're home, you can make some of those promotional tours your editor has been requesting," he said.

"Maybe. What do you plan to do?"

"We'll stay at Mom and Dad's for a while. Until we see how Dad does. Then see about getting a place of our own."

"I can give notice to the tenants, we could live in my house," she offered, almost holding her breath.

Was he serious about not ending their relationship as soon as possible? Would he consider several months together before he left? It'd help him with the financial end of things. Maybe she should mention that.

"How much notice do you have to give?" Keith asked.

"A month."

"That might work."

She let her breath out slowly. At least he was agreeable to staying together for another month and maybe longer.

You're like a sister to me.

The words echoed again and again as Drea stared unseeingly out across the sparkling water far below them. She never wanted to be his sister.

Maybe it was time she made sure he knew that.

She had at least a month while she stayed with him at his parents' place. Could she use that time to make Keith aware of her as a woman, as a real wife?

Make him as aware of her as she was of him?

Make him want her the way a man wanted a woman?

If he'd just give them a chance, they could make a real marriage, share a life together. Be happy.

They were happy in Kuwait.

But he still saw the betrayal and ruin caused by his first wife. He was blinded to the possible joy of marriage.

Could she change his mind?

He said they needn't split when they returned to the States, but she knew he'd be caught up in starting up his own business and helping out with his father's company. Too busy to fall in love with his wife.

She'd have to act fast if she was to have a chance at happy ever after.

She'd hoped to effect a change during the years in Kuwait,

but that was impossible now. And the past year hadn't really made a difference.

Would anything have changed in the next two?

Time was of the essence. She had one last shot at a lifetime of happiness with the man she loved.

She could do it or die trying. She was no longer going to worry about upsetting the status quo. She'd give it her all. If their marriage ended, it wouldn't be for lack of trying on her part.

And if nothing worked, she had some wonderful memories to sustain her. She wouldn't have traded one day of the past year with Keith for anything. Except to have him notice her, want her as she wanted him. Love her.

He didn't have a clue. She'd never known she was such a good actress, able to hide her feelings for so long. She didn't care to think of what would have happened if she'd told him that she loved him as she'd been tempted to do on so many occasions.

He'd abided by their agreement—the least she could do was the same.

But they weren't in Kuwait any longer.

And she no longer wished to abide by the terms.

"I never thanked you for all you've done, Drea. You never complained, you never whined to go home for a visit. You didn't mind that we lived frugally in order to save money," Keith said as the plane began its descent into JFK.

"I've been happy, Keith. I never lacked for anything. And why would I want to go home? I have nothing there. Daddy was the last of my family. Besides, I consider you part of my family now, brother dear."

He looked startled. His eyes narrowed. "What does that mean?"

She smiled, let him consider that.

"You think of me as your sister. I should start thinking of you as the brother I never had."

She almost laughed at the thought. She could never think of him as her brother.

He frowned as if not liking her comment. It was no more than the truth, but for some reason it seemed bothered him.

That alone gave Drea hope.

"I need to make a list of all the things we should do," she said primly.

He chuckled, remembering all the times in Kuwait she'd whipped out a notebook to jot something down so she wouldn't forget.

"You and your lists. You make more than anyone I know."

"I can't keep track of everything if I don't. You know that."

"I know that for the past year you made lists of everything, from groceries, to birthday presents for friends and my family, to which chapter you were going to write and what would go into it. Never saw such a woman for lists," he teased. "And all mixed together, too. How do you keep them straight?"

She smiled at the shared memories.

"Writers get absentminded when thinking up plots. Lists keep me on track."

She liked his gentle teasing. His eyes grew silver and his face relaxed. So often during the past year he'd fallen into a bitter dark mood. She knew when this happened there was nothing to do but wait until his mood passed.

Would he ever forget and move on?

Once through customs, Keith found a restaurant, where they ate a hearty breakfast. Wandering around the airport, more to pass time than from any real interest, they finally found the gate for their final leg.

Sitting near the door to the jetway, Drea drew out her notebook and began jotting down things she needed to do when they were back in Norfolk.

When Keith went to buy a newspaper, Drea stared at her notebook. She was going to plan her attack and having a list would help her. This was one objective she wouldn't leave to chance. There was a limited opportunity and she needed to make the most of every moment.

She tried to think of what she could do to entice her husband. For the first time she rather wished she'd been a romance writer instead of writing mysteries. Maybe then she'd have boatloads of ideas for seducing a man.

She sighed, staring off into space as she tried to plot Keith's downfall.

Chapter Three

By late afternoon, they'd arrived at the Branson's home. Neither parent was home, both were at the hospital, but Judy Branson, Keith's mother, had left a welcoming note, including the fact she'd made up the bed in his bedroom with fresh linens.

"I wasn't expecting this," Drea said, waving a vague hand toward the queen-size bed she saw when she entered the bedroom with her carry-on bag. Staring at it, she tried to think.

It sat oddly amid the mementos of Keith's boyhood room. The trophies, pennants, battered books stacked on the bookshelves and on the scarred desk, displayed interests over a decade old. His mother had changed nothing in his room since he'd moved out.

Except for the totally unexpected new bed.

"It's about time we consummated this marriage, don't you think, darling? I'm glad Mom surprised us with the bed. I've wanted you desperately this past year. Don't cover that luscious body of yours another minute."

She glanced up at him, wishing for the millionth time that the dialogue she wrote in her head would actually come from his mouth.

Leaning back against the doorjamb, he watched her with

lazy humor. His arms crossed over his chest, the muscles bulged beneath his cotton shirt. His hair had bleached almost white from the hot Kuwait sun, while his skin had tanned as dark as teak. The combination threw his sparkling gray eyes into prominence.

She often felt as if she were drowning in those wonderful cool eyes.

She frowned, not liking the amusement she saw. Turning back to her carry-on bag, she plopped it on the bed, wondering how they were going to handle things tonight.

They'd been delayed leaving JFK due to mechanical difficulties and it had been later than anticipated when they reached Norfolk. With so little sleep on the plane, she felt exhausted. She wanted nothing so much as to get in bed and sleep until morning.

"I'm so tired and you look like you got up a few minutes ago," she grumbled.

Her eyes felt as if they were filled with all the sand on Virginia Beach. Her body ached with fatigue–it was still on Kuwait time, whatever that was.

"You're cranky because you're tired. What are you trying to do to your clothes, scramble them like eggs?" His voice was calm, soothing.

"I'm looking for something to sleep in. And I wasn't expecting to share a bed."

Not after all this time. Not after fantasizing about it every night in their apartment in Kuwait. It seemed as if dreams did come true, in a way.

"Let's not bother with clothes, let's just slip beneath the sheets

and—"

"I didn't know she bought the bed for us. The last night I slept in this room it had bunk beds," he said patiently. "And with Dad in the hospital, I sure didn't expect Mom to be thinking of us and the bunk beds."

She glanced up. "I'm so tired I can hardly see straight," she murmured, returning to rummaging through her bag to see if she could find something halfway decent to wear to sleep. If she didn't get into bed soon, she'd drop where she stood.

Maybe that was the answer. She'd sleep in her clothes in a puddle on the floor beside the bed.

"Here." He tossed a soft white T-shirt across the expanse of mattress. "Wear this tonight and tomorrow we'll see what other arrangement we can make."

She held the shirt up in front of her. It'd easily cover her to mid thigh. For a brief moment she picture him wearing it. He often left for work wearing a white T-shirt with his soft, faded jeans and tough work boots.

She vividly remembered how his muscular body filled out the shirtt. It would swim on her.

Involuntarily she glanced back at the bed. It was better than nothing.

And it sure looked as if he wasn't going to use the words she'd hoped he'd say. Not that he ever had, even when she'd fantasized in Kuwait. She sighed. A telepath she was not.

"It's a big bed, Drea, and we're both so tired we won't even know the other's in it. Go to sleep, honey. I'll go and wait for Mom to get home. I'll come back up later."

Drea watched her husband of eleven months leave the bedroom.

"Maybe you won't know I'm in it, but I'll sure know you're there," she said softly after the door clicked behind him.

If she weren't so tired, she'd appreciate the irony of the situation. For over a decade she'd wanted Keith. And for most of that time he hadn't even been aware of her or only saw her as his sister's friend.

Be careful what you wish for, went the old saying. Now she knew why. The reality was not at all the way she'd pictured it.

She drew the T-shirt up to her face, rubbing it gently against her cheek. It smelled of outdoors and soap. Was there a hint of his scent?

Moving her carry-on off the bed, she quickly stripped down and donned the soft cotton shirt. It flowed over her skin like a caress. She smiled, knowing it had once covered Keith like a second skin. For a moment she almost imagined warmth from his body.

Slipping beneath the sheet, she switched off the bedside light, leaving on the one by his side. Her body ached she was so tired. It wasn't easy traveling from Kuwait to Virginia all in one day. Especially with the uncertainty and worry they faced because of Keith's father's unexpected heart attack.

And the worry about her own future.

Tomorrow there'd be so much to deal with. But for now she relished the soft mattress, the clean sheets.

In only seconds Drea fell fast asleep.

Slowly, consciousness seeped in. Heat enveloped her. Cranky, she wondered if the air conditioner had stopped working again. The reliability of the electricity in Kuwait left much to be desired. You'd think that a country that had so much oil—

Her eyes flew open.

She wasn't in Kuwait any longer. She was home. Or rather, back in Virginia. But it was still hot.

She shifted slightly, hitting the hard muscles behind her, feeling a heavy weight across her waist. Slowly she turned her head. Keith lay right beside her, his arm heavy across her waist. It was his body heat that woke her, enveloped her.

For a long moment Drea held her breath. Sliding and turning until she lay flat on her back, she studied him.

He was sound asleep, his breathing deep and even. Tracing his much-loved features gently with her eyes, she stored the memory.

Her only time sleeping with her husband. She wouldn't forget a single aspect, from his tousled and mussed sun-streaked hair to his dark lashes lying like shadow crescents against his tanned cheeks; from the stubborn chin to his arched eyebrows. The rough stubble of his beard beckoned. She longed to run her fingertips across his jaw, feel the slight roughness she knew she'd find.

He looked even bigger in bed than when standing. Or maybe he seemed bigger because he was so close. His hand rested against her, heavy, tantalizing. He was sprawled over most of the bed, including her side.

A fierce longing rose within her. She wanted him so much

she almost trembled. Closing her eyes, she turned away, willing the strength that'd held her in good stead throughout the past year to remain strong enough to endure this morning. She wished she knew enough to seduce him. Wished she was experienced enough to entice him to make passionate love to her at least once before they split.

She'd so like to have one glorious memory to take with her down the long, lonely road that stretched out before her if her plan to make him fall in love with her didn't work.

When would he tell her goodbye? She'd done as he'd asked—married him so he could work in Kuwait. While the time they agreed to wasn't officially over, their assignment in Kuwait had ended. She knew they were back in Virginia for good.

Their marriage was no longer required.

She sighed, pressing her palm against her breast as if that could assuage the ache that spread. She'd cherished every moment together. She thought she'd have more, thought she'd have three full years.

"Awake?"

His voice was a low murmur in her ear, his breath a gentle breeze against her cheek.

Spinning back, she gazed into his deep gray eyes. Flushing with the close proximity, with the intensity of feeling she always experienced around him, she nodded shyly.

She wished her heart didn't catch every time he looked at her. Wished after all these years she could ignore the tingling sensation being near him always brought. Wished she saw him as no more than her friend Becky's older brother.

"Sleep enough?" he asked, his eyes lazy in the early morning, his body still relaxed.

"I guess. I woke up without an alarm."

Her heart rate increased. His solid presence only inches from her disturbed her, his hand resting on her sent shivering waves of sensation that splashed through her as they heated her blood.

Did he realize he touched her so intimately?

She wished she dared move beneath his hand, push it up—

"What time is it?" she asked almost desperately.

He shrugged. "I don't know and don't want to move to see the clock. Not too early, the sun's well up."

"What time are you going to the hospital?"

She couldn't believe they were having an ordinary conversation while they were lying in bed. She was wearing only a T-shirt. Had Keith worn anything? His chest was bare, the sheet stopping at his waist. Curiosity rose. Was he wearing anything at all beneath the sheet?

"Mom said visiting hours start at eleven. We'll go then."

"You want me to go, too?"

"Of course." He frowned. "You're my wife. Dad'll want to see you, too. Don't you want to go?"

"Yes. I just wasn't sure."

Even now the memory of the evening after her father's funeral was vividly etched in her mind, every detail as clear as if it'd happened yesterday.

"I guess I thought since we'd end the marriage now that we're back, you wouldn't want to keep up the pretense of a happy marriage. We won't be returning to Kuwait, will we?"

He shook his head. "I doubt it. I'll know more after we see Dad and I can judge how things stand with the business. We agreed to give the appearance of a normal marriage to stop any questions. I don't want to change that now. I told you yesterday we didn't need to separate just because we've returned home."

"No?"

"Not yet, anyway. You didn't see my mother last night. She's a nervous wreck. She's always depended so much on Dad. Now she's going to need us until he's well again. And I don't think Dad needs any more upsets until he's recovered. They think this marriage is solid. I don't want to change that."

"And our separating would be upsetting."

It made sense.

The Bransons had been delighted when Keith announced their marriage. She'd practically been a part of their family since she was a teenager. They'd welcomed her even more fervently in light of Keith's disastrous first marriage.

They'd be disappointed when they separated.

Though she wished he wanted to stay married for different reasons.

"You remember how ecstatic they were when we married. A lot more enthusiastic than they ever were with Diane. I certainly don't want to do anything now to jeopardize Dad's recovery or Mom's mental state. We stay married until he's well again."

"That could be a couple of months," she said slowly.

What if she didn't want to stay married any longer? The

bargain had been while they were in Kuwait. How like him to assume she'd do his bidding, just because she'd pretty much always done so.

"Or even longer. Don't worry, we'll keep the same arrangement. I'll support you, you work on your writing."

The same arrangement? What about sharing a bed?

"I'm starting to make money with the books now so I don't need your support—"

"Don't argue. I said I'd support you while we were married. When we split, you'll need that money. You won't be getting anything else from me. That was our bargain."

"Except help to get reestablished, remember?" she said, hurt afresh by his reminder of their prenuptial agreement.

She grew more and more tired of reaping the results of Diane's sowing.

"Yes. How much will that cost me?" he asked cynically.

"I've thought about it. I won't need money from you actually. I have my house. I'll give the tenants notice right away and be able to move back in by the time your father's well."

"You've thought it all out." He frowned.

"It wasn't much to think about. It's what we agreed to last summer. The timetable just moved up a bit. Instead of three years, now it'll be sooner. You should be delighted."

"I'm not sure I like talking about ending things. I liked coming home to you in Kuwait, telling you about work, eating the meals you always had ready. True, we no longer need the marriage for the same reason if we don't return to Kuwait, but there'll be time enough later to discuss ending it."

"If you like. I'll need some help from you, however," she

said hesitantly, glancing at him from beneath lowered lashes.

This was it. If he showed no reaction or if he eagerly agreed, she'd know she hadn't a chance.

"Whatever you need, let me know."

"Dating."

"What?"

That was obviously the last thing he'd expected to hear.

"Dating. You know, how to play the game. How to start scintillating conversations. How to get someone interested in me. Basic instruction in how to entice a man."

Chapter Four

Keith rose up on one elbow, leaned over her, his eyes hard. "What are you talking about?"

Drea met his gaze fearlessly, secretly intrigued that he showed so much reaction.

"I'm talking about you teaching me how to attract a man. During this past year I discovered I like being married. Only next time I want to share the bedroom, as well. I don't want another platonic relationship. I didn't date much when I was younger."

No need to let him know she'd always hoped he'd ask her out.

And the dates she'd gone on hadn't proved very successful because she compared every man to Keith.

"Then the last two years of my Dad's life I spent pretty much all my free time with him because he was so sick. Then you and I started our fake marriage. So I'm way out of practice."

"We're sharing a bed now," he muttered, still glaring at her. "You're still married. If you didn't want a platonic relationship, all you had to do was tell me."

"Keith," she said gently, firmly removing his hand from

her body before she threw herself into his arms and begged him to make love to her.

"I've done all you asked in this marriage. I'll even stay married a little longer, even though we're no longer in Kuwait, in order to help you out with your folks. But you said you'd help me when we split. You promised. I've decided I like being married, being part of a couple. I'm calling in your marker. You need to help me find a husband."

He lay back and stared at the ceiling. His quiet, shy little librarian-turned-author wife had totally shocked him. Drea had always seemed so content working at the library, living with her dad. He knew from Becky that she didn't date much.

She'd been the perfect wife during their time in Kuwait, always cheerful, always ready to do whatever he suggested– from last-minute dinners with fellow construction workers to accommodating his long, irregular hours. She hadn't asked for much.

Until now.

Now she expected his help in finding her a husband.

If he wasn't so against marriage, he'd stay married to her himself. She was fun to be around, easy to talk to and could cook like a dream. Maybe they should stay married.

Closing his eyes, he swore softly.

That had to be the most foolish idea he'd ever come up with.

He was through with marriage. He refused to get tangled up with another woman and risk losing everything a second time. They'd made their agreement.

And he had promised to help her. So he would, if that was

what she really wanted. *Blast it all!*

"I'll take a quick shower and then you can have the bathroom," Drea said, taking advantage of Keith's silence.

She hastened across the hallway and closed the bathroom door behind her, leaning against it for a long moment. She felt almost giddy with relief and surging hope. Many more seconds in close proximity with him like that and she'd become a babbling fool.

He was so clueless. She'd loved him for over a decade, since the first time she'd seen him when she'd come over to visit Becky after moving into the neighborhood. And he didn't have an inkling.

Turning on the shower, she tried to think of more mundane things. Reveling in the warm water that cascaded over her, she plunged gleefully beneath the strong shower. The amenities in Kuwait had been less than first-class.

She let the water soothe her. She needed the relaxation to spark her creativity. Once again she wished she'd tried writing romances instead of mysteries. She knew forty-three ways to poison someone without leaving a trace, but hadn't a clue how to seduce one stubborn, arrogant, sexy man who believed that all women were out to get him.

Win or lose, she was determined to make Keith Branson see her as a desirable woman at least once before they separated.

He could point out what he liked in a woman, while ostensibly trying to help her find a new husband. Would she match any of his criteria?

One night—that's all she asked. Was it too much?

She'd resigned herself to being alone years ago. Knowing he saw her as a friend of his sister, she knew he'd never fall passionately, lastingly in love with her. But she'd so much like to have one special night before they separated.

Yeah, and maybe pigs would fly.

It was worth a try, she argued. She had nothing to lose. If she didn't do something, and soon, she'd find herself alone again.

Knowing Keith, he'd never have asked her to marry him if he hadn't needed a wife in Kuwait. Once single again, she doubted he'd ever remarry. She'd hoped being the supportive wife in Kuwait would demonstrate that he needed her in his life.

But he'd been too caught up in work to even notice her. As soon as his father was on the road to recovery, Keith would stick to the original plan to end their marriage.

She was sorry his father had that heart attack, but it kept them together a bit longer. Whatever the reason, she'd gained a reprieve.

Time to change tactics. Obviously the ones she'd tried up to now hadn't worked. She still had a few weeks. She was determined to seduce that sexy man or die trying.

Finished with her shower, Drea dried herself off and pulled on the T-shirt. Wrapping a fresh towel like a turban around her long wet hair, she slipped back across the hall into their bedroom.

After a year of separate bedrooms, to be expected to share one had startled her last night. Now, maybe it would turn out to be the best thing. Especially since she planned to start her new seduce-her-husband campaign immediately.

Keith leaned back against the headboard when she returned, his gaze running down her body, his expression unreadable as he studied her. She tried to ignore the flash of heat that burst deep inside and treat their situation as normally as she could.

Was she actress enough?

"The bathroom's all yours," she said easily, going to her suitcase and rummaging around again, looking for clean underwear and the dress she'd wear today. It'd have to be ironed. After being packed for two days, everything in the suitcase would be wrinkled beyond belief.

"Thanks."

Keith found he didn't want to leave. He wanted to stay and see if she'd get dressed in front of him. He wanted to snatch away that towel and see her blond hair settle over her shoulders, wet and straight. He knew it'd dry soft and wavy.

She appeared so self-contained, so self-assured, it annoyed him.

He'd like to rattle her a bit, shake her up the way she'd shaken him up with her request that he help her find a husband.

After all these years he thought he knew Drea, but was beginning to discover he hadn't a clue.

Was she as devious as Diane had been?

Was he going to find the quiet, sweet woman he'd married had a different agenda?

For a moment the old bitterness rose. He'd never let her or any woman manipulate him again. When his dad recovered, they'd separate, get the annulment. They'd agreed to do that a year ago and he'd make sure they followed through.

Only…he was second guessing the final terms.

And he sure didn't like her request that he help her find another man. Would she be as sweet and generous with another guy as she'd been with him this past year living in the heat and hardships of Kuwait?

Once or twice he'd almost brought up the idea of sharing a bed. But he'd honored the terms of their agreement and never broached the subject.

Now she was proposing to find another man.

Keith didn't like the situation at all.

Rising reluctantly, he drew on his jeans and hunted for clothes to wear after his shower. Normally he slept in the nude, but had worn briefs last night out of consideration for Drea.

He smiled grimly. That'd been another shock, to find he liked to cuddle up with her, feel her honey heat against his skin.

Not going to go there!

Without another word, he stomped out of the bedroom and headed for the bathroom. After living with her for a year, was he now starting to desire his wife?

His timing sucked.

In seconds he returned. He'd forgotten his shaving kit. He was lucky he could remember his way to the bathroom after her shocking announcement. He wanted to stay and—

He stopped, poleaxed. Desire hit Keith low down, hot and hard. He stared at her. They'd been married almost a year and this was the first time he'd seen her undressed.

Quickly he scanned her slender frame. She was incredibly lovely. Why hadn't he noticed before now?

Drea had donned French-cut bikini panties that accentuated her long, tanned legs. The lace revealed more than it concealed. The skimpy covering was a shock—if he thought about he would have expected plain white cotton briefs.

She paused momentarily when he burst back into the room, then resumed pulling on a matching bra. The wild lavender color complemented her honey-gold skin. The smooth globes of her breasts were high and firm and stained a pale pink with her embarrassment.

Keith couldn't look away. Even covered with the pale lace and satin, he wanted to touch her all over. Feel that satiny skin. Stunned at the reaction, he raised his gaze to clash with Drea's.

Drea fastened her bra while holding Keith's gaze. Her heart pounded as she fought for control. With an show of indifference she was far from feeling, she slowly drew the towel from around her hair, then shook the strands free. Her heart was pumping as if she'd run a race. She felt his eyes on her like a hot brand. Determined to ignore the shivering sensations that shook her, she took a deep breath and willed her voice to come out normal.

"Does your mother have an iron I can use?" she said.

If he didn't stop looking at her like he was going to eat her up, she'd melt down right where she stood. Heat licked through her. She wanted to throw herself against him. But she held her ground, tilting her chin slightly, fighting the urge to cover herself. Maybe this was exactly the kind of thing he needed to wake up to the fact she was a desirable woman.

"I never knew you were so lovely, so beautiful all over. Just let me feast my eyes on your beauty. Oh, my love, I want you so badly."

"Yeah, sure. Mom has one in the laundry room. I'll get it," he said.

Man, he had to get out of here before he forgot all about going to the hospital to see his dad, forgot about his mother's need for support and tossed Drea on their rumpled bed and kissed her senseless.

Then make love to her all day long.

"Thanks," she replied sweetly, smiling at him.

Her voice was breathless and something about it inflamed him. Her eyes glittered softly in the morning light as she flickered them his way, then ignored him as she finished fastening the bra. She was so pretty. Was he only realizing that now? She wouldn't have any trouble finding a man.

Jealousy flared. Frowning, Keith turned away. He'd get the blasted iron and then take a shower. A cold shower.

Drea watched him leave, disappointed once again that he hadn't said the words she'd so wanted him to say. Sighing softly, she turned to make the bed. Even standing almost naked before him had no effect.

Scrap a striptease to tantalize him—obviously that didn't have the slightest impact. Was there anything she could do?

Keith returned with an iron and ironing board. He seemed frustrated. Drea thanked him and watched as he slammed their door behind him. Two seconds later he opened it again and stormed over to his suitcase and snatched up his shaving kit. Without looking at her, he left, slamming the door behind him a second time.

Slowly she began to smile.

So maybe there'd been some effect after all.

By the time they were ready to leave for the hospital, Drea had thought through various steps she'd take to make this husband of hers take notice. She'd jotted them down on her ever-present notepad. She'd have to fine-tune the plan as she went, but it was a start.

First she needed to show him all the things she did that made her indispensable. Show him she was as different from Diane as night was from day.

Second, she needed to show him she didn't need him for money. Her first book had sold extremely well. Her second was already out and her publisher expected even higher sales. And the third was in the publishing queue.

Not that Keith had ever shown an interest in her writing, beyond inquiring how the day-to-day work at the computer had gone. Would he be surprised at her success? Would that change the way he saw her?

She certainly wasn't a gambler the way Diane was. And she didn't have a lover on the side.

She paused at the kitchen door. She wasn't going to bribe him. She'd get him to acknowledge an attraction between them before telling him of her success. He still needed money to reestablish himself in the construction business. She needed to make sure he cared for her alone, and not what financial support she could add.

She'd loved him for so long she couldn't stand it if he

didn't even care slightly for her. She'd been truthful when she'd told him she liked being married—but only to him. Would he let her go? Would he offer pointers to get back into dating?

If so, her case was hopeless.

She could only wait and see what Keith did.

Matt Branson was still in the cardiac care unit and permitted only one visitor at a time and only for a few minutes. His wife went to see him when the three of them arrived at the hospital. Keith and Drea went into the waiting area. The room had a large window that overlooked the hospital grounds. The chairs were standard institutional issue.

"This must be hard for you," Keith said as he sat on one of the chairs, facing the window, remembering Drea's father had been in this same hospital when he died. She sank down beside him gazing out the window, nodding.

Old memories surfaced. She remembered being here a year ago. Only her father had been too sick to recover.

She hoped the outcome would be different for Keith's dad.

When he reached over to take her cold hand, she looked at him, startled by his touch. She didn't think he'd touched her more than a couple of times during their entire stay in Kuwait. But since hearing about his father, he'd held her on the plane, held her last night, and now this.

Lacing his fingers with hers, he rested their linked hands on his hard thigh.

"I'm sure your father will be all right," she said, wanting to comfort him, confused by his actions. He'd never held hands with her before.

"We'll have more information when we talk to his doctor. Mom said he felt Dad was as strong as he was going to get for the surgery. They don't want to delay any longer. I feel so helpless, like I ought to be able to do something. What if he doesn't recover? He's not an old man, only fifty-eight."

"Your mom said he'd been in bad health for quite some time."

"So she said, but he hid it. Which is just like him. He always was a strong man. I thought of him as invincible."

"Then this illness will prove doubly hard for him. He'll need you around even more than your mom does, I think," Drea said. "You'll have to run the business while he's recovering. He trusts you and won't worry if you're in charge. You know it's going to take him a long time to get better."

Keith eyed her oddly. "You expect me to step in and run my father's business?"

"Who else?" She shrugged. "Someone has to do it. You worked with him before you went out on your own. He never wanted you to go, you know. He always wanted it to be Branson and Son. He'll leave it to you one day."

"Think so?" His voice cooled noticeably.

She nodded, puzzled by his tone. "Of course. You must know it, too. Good heavens, Keith, you worked for him every summer through high school and college. Started out with him when you got your engineering degree. You know he always wanted you in business with him."

"He and I lasted less than a year when I worked full-time for him. He wants to do large tracts of houses, condos or fancy apartments. I want to do custom homes, put a lot of craftsmanship into them, make them distinctive and unique. We never agreed on anything when I worked for him."

She shrugged. "It won't matter now. You'll be in charge until he's back. Time enough then to see if you want to stay or go off on your own again once he's better. But my guess is that he'll want you to stay, maybe make you a full partner."

"If he did, I'd be set again. I wouldn't have to worry about starting over, wouldn't have to work my way back up."

'I'd need someone with me to help me. You, Drea, I need you. Please say you'll stay with me. Forget our plans for an annulment. Be my forever wife."

"You'd like that, wouldn't you? It'd mean instant success, instant wealth. But don't forget our bargain—you get nothing when we split." His voice was cool, remote.

She started as if he'd slapped her.

Yanking her hand free of his, she rose and turned to glare at him, hands on her hips, leaning over him to make sure he could look no farther than her face.

"Listen to me, you arrogant idiot, I do not want anything from you!" *Except your love, which you won't ever give.* "It must be extremely wearing to believe the whole female population is against you. Well, I've got news for you, buster, this is one female who'll count herself lucky when this farce of a marriage is over. Of all the opinionated, self-centered, dumb males I've ever known, you take the cake. Yes, you got a raw deal with Diane, but not all women are like Diane. But you go ahead and wallow in that self pity you love so much and ignore everyone who might genuinely be interested in you, who might want to help you."

"What? No protestations of undying love? You weren't so reticent as a teenager. I practically had to beat you off with a stick," he retorted, stung by her words.

Chapter Five

She stood upright, knowing the color drained from her face. How nasty of him to remind her of her crush when she'd first met him. She knew she'd been blatantly chasing him, but she'd only been sixteen.

She'd taken great pains to hide her feelings from him once she'd overheard him laughing about her with some of his buddies. She'd been crushed.

She couldn't seem to help loving the man, but she sure didn't have to let him know it.

Tilting her chin, she glared at him.

"That was a long time ago, Keith. You should be so lucky to have me love you now."

With that she turned and stalked away.

She'd wait in the hall outside Matt's room for her turn to visit, then leave and check on the situation with her house.

For the first time in hours the thought of staying with Keith was not uppermost in her mind.

In fact, she wondered how she continued to love him when he was so impossible.

Keith rubbed his face as he watched her storm away. Blast it all, he hadn't meant to insult her. He must be suffering from jet lag.

Was that her excuse?

What was the matter with her? Ever since they'd arrived last night Drea had changed. Gone was the quiet, shy woman he'd known for years. Instead, he was being treated to a tempting, sexy female.

Which was the real Drea? The quiet friend of his sister he'd lived with this past year or the hotheaded, provocative woman of this morning?

It must be jet lag.

He admitted to himself he shouldn't have made the crack about her crush on him as a teenager. Truth to tell, at the time he'd been flattered. She'd been a pretty girl even then. But she was his younger sister's friend, and he hadn't wanted to be razzed by his buddies, so he'd laughed it away.

After a few months, she'd stayed away. She'd stopped coming after him, had virtually ignored him in the years that followed.

The teenage crush had play itself out and she'd moved on.

She hadn't come to his wedding to Diane, though she and her father had been invited. Not that it mattered. Thinking about Diane put him in a bad mood. If she hadn't been such a compulsive gambler, hiding the fact before their marriage, discounting its importance in her life after their wedding, he'd not be in the financial situation he was in today.

And if she hadn't been such a cheat, he might still be married to her.

Instead she'd taken off with a man who had much more wealth than she'd ever see with Keith.

Idly he wondered if she had run through that man's

money yet.

Why hadn't he been more attune to the possibilities of problems with Diane? He'd had enough problems before when dealing with the opposite sex. From Sara in high school to Bonnie in college to Diane, his track record was appalling.

His experience let him know Drea'd be no different. She only wanted him for her own gain. If he hadn't offered to support her to build her writing career, she wouldn't have married him. For all her fancy talk, that was the bottom line.

Keith shifted his gaze out the window, thinking about what he and Drea had discussed.

Would his father want Keith to assume control of Branson Construction until he recovered?

What if he never recovered sufficiently to return to the helm? For a long, dark moment Keith considered the various ramifications.

He wanted his father's full recovery. Business was secondary.

He could run Branson Construction, but if he did it long term, he'd want to make changes.

He'd finish out the contracts they now had, but if his father wasn't ready to return to work by then, Keith would move into the custom home market.

Maybe do both custom work and the cookie-cutter developments his father preferred.

He must be getting older—now he was thinking compromise.

He smiled grimly and shook his head. What would Drea

think?

He quickly pushed the thought from his mind. She wouldn't be part of his life after the next few weeks. Or only as a family friend. It didn't matter what she thought.

For one brief second he hoped his father would take months to recover. That'd mean that Drea would stay around and they could continue as they had in Kuwait. No sense rushing to separate.

Drea spent her allotted five minutes with her father-in-law. Secretly appalled at how bad he looked, with all the tubes and wires connecting him to various machines, she gave a good performance of how pleased she was to see him and how glad she was to be home.

Fortunately, there wasn't much time to talk and she escaped gladly, lest she give something away to indicate that everything wasn't going as well in her marriage as the older Bransons thought.

"Drea?" A young woman met her in the hall when she left the room.

"Becky! Oh, I'm so glad to see you!"

Drea flung her arms around her longtime friend and hugged her hard.

"I'm so sorry about your dad, but he seems in good spirits and that's the important thing. I'm sure he'll come through the surgery with flying colors," she said when she stepped back.

"I hope so. It's been so hard. I'm glad you and Keith came back. Where is he, in with Dad?"

Becky wasn't as tall as Drea. Slender with hair a shade darker than her brother's she looked good in her light cotton dress. She was also seven months pregnant.

"He's in the waiting room. I just finished my visit with your dad. We're doing it one at a time, you know. Your mom went first, of course. Did you want to see him now?"

"Let Keith visit first. I'm so glad to see you. And glad you both came home for this. It's been hard with mom feeling like her world's falling apart. Tell me everything. Your emails were sporadic, at best. I thought you were a writer."

Linking arms with her best friend, Becky headed toward the small waiting room.

Drea smiled at her friend's comment.

"By the time I finished working on my book every day, I was too tired to think about writing any thing. Besides, life in Kuwait was so routine you knew everything we did after my first email. I tried to find new things to talk about, but really there was only so many ways I could tell you about shopping at the market. I must say, you didn't exactly flood my inbox with emails."

"Same excuse then, you know how boring life here can be. Plus I don't have a way with words like you do. I'd much rather talk in person!"

They walked down the hall to the waiting room.

"Keith!"

Becky rushed over to hug her brother when they reached the waiting room.

"I'm so glad to see you! It's your turn to see Dad. I'll visit when you're done. It's good to have you back."

Keith gave his sister a hug. "It's good to see you. How're Tom and the boys? Were you as large as this with the last two?" he teased with a wide grin.

She wrinkled her nose at him.

"Yep. Tom and the boys are fine. Wait until you see Tyler. He's grown so much you won't recognize him. And Trevor's in preschool."

Slyly she glanced around at Drea. "Any interesting announcements you two have to make? All in the family, so to speak?"

Drea smiled and shook her head, hoping the ache in her heart didn't reflect in her expression. She'd love to have a child with Keith. Being an only child herself, she'd always longed to be part of a large family.

Now that her father and mother were both gone, she wished for a family even more.

Another foolish dream that might never come true.

She wanted to be the mother of Keith's children and he was still talking annulment.

Keith answered briskly with a quick glance at Drea "No, we're not planning a family right now. I'll talk to you after I see Dad."

Becky watched him walk away with surprise, then swung her gaze to Drea.

"I can understand not wanting to have a kid in Kuwait, but aren't you two here for good? Or will you be going back to Kuwait?"

"I believe Keith ended the contract he had with the company, planning to be here to help however he can for a long as it takes until your dad's back on his feet."

She sidestepped the issue by asking "Did you bring

pictures of the boys? I can't believe Tyler is over two."

"Well, I just happen to have a couple of recent pictures."

Becky sat down beside Drea and pulled out her phone. In only seconds they were scanning through the dozens of pictures of Becky's boys.

Drea gazed at them longingly. She yearned to have a little boy. Or a little girl. It didn't matter, she'd love any baby she had.

Sighing softly, her determination grew stronger. She wanted to prove to her stubborn husband that she'd continue to make him an excellent wife–and not just until his father recovered. He deserved some happiness after the heartache Diane had put him through.

Together they deserved a loving family and she wondered what she could do to give them a chance. Being the perfect wife in Kuwait hadn't been enough.

Would the intimacy of sharing a room make a difference?

"That enough about my kids. You and Keith will have to come over in a couple of days and see them. And Tom. But tell me about your writing. We were so thrilled when *Open the Gate to Death* hit the best-seller list. That was unexpected, wasn't it?

"Yes. Especially for a first book. My publisher did a great job with publicity."

Nonsense. You did a great job writing the book. I loved it, and *Killer Instinct*. Isn't that one on the bestseller right now? I've already pre-ordered *Mocking Death Again*. I can't wait for it to be released."

Drea smiled at her friend. "I'm honored. You didn't have

to buy a book—I'd give you one, silly."

"I wanted to help establish your bestselling record. What does Keith think of all this?"

"Actually, he doesn't, um, know about it. He was so busy in Kuwait. The project turned out to be very demanding…" Drea trailed off.

It was hard to explain exactly why she hadn't shared every triumph with him.

Some of it had to do with the reason for their agreement. Drea also didn't want him to think she was bragging or trying to impress him with her success.

Truth be told, she'd been amazed at how much money she'd made on her first book. And the advance on the next two had been astonishing.

Somehow she'd thought knowing all that would make him feel differently toward her and she hadn't wanted to risk it.

And it'd been so easy to keep silent in Kuwait. He never asked and they weren't surrounded by people who mentioned her books.

Now she wasn't so sure keeping quiet had been a good idea. She should tell him. She didn't want him to hear about it from someone else.

Which he might, especially if Becky set herself up to be a one-woman cheering section.

Becky stared at her in astonishment.

"How busy is too busy? What did that have to do with anything? It'd only take two seconds to say my book hit the New York Times best-seller list."

Drea shrugged, wishing she'd anticipated this. If Becky

knew what her agent was working on now, she'd go through the roof.

And she was right, Drea needed to let her husband know before Becky spilled the beans.

"It didn't seem so important over in Kuwait. I only knew about it myself because of your emails and my agent's. It felt nebulous, like it wasn't real or something. I'll tell him."

"How can you say it wasn't important? Good grief, girl, the New York Times list! Just when were you planning to tell him?" Becky demanded.

Drea smiled, remembering how Becky always liked things done instantly.

"Soon."

Becky stared at her strangely.

"You know," she said slowly, "I've often wondered over the past year what happened between you and Keith that caused you to get married so quickly. He seemed so bitter after the divorce with Diane. Then your father died and the next thing I knew you two were married and moving to Kuwait."

"It wasn't that sudden. You came to the wedding."

Becky shook her head. "If you could call it that. A hurried affair at the courthouse. I remember you always dreamed about a large wedding with all our friends and a beautiful dress."

"I know, but when Daddy died, I didn't feel the same," Drea said.

She'd have loved a big wedding, but without her father, the dream had lost its luster.

And of course their marriage was only a business

arrangement. No need for the expense of a fancy wedding for that.

She sighed. Life took funny turns.

Chapter Six

Keith came out of his father room and leaned back against the wall, staring at the ceiling as if for answers. He hadn't been prepared. His dad looked far worse than he'd expected. He needed to talk to the doctor and get a realistic assessment of the probability of his father's recovery.

And he wanted a realistic estimated of the length of time for his convalescence if complete recovery was in the picture.

Keith wasn't at all sure his dad would be back at work as soon as he first thought.

It looked as if Drea's assessment was on the mark. He'd be heading up Branson Construction for the foreseeable future. His dad had asked him to do that just now.

Not that they'd had much chance to talk. Even with the oxygen, he had difficulty speaking without gasping for breath. But he'd been insistent in getting Keith to agree to take over.

Keith reassured him he'd do so and confirmed he wasn't going back to Kuwait.

He'd swing by the current job site today and see how things stood. The office was in the portable trailer that went from job site to job site. He'd come up to speed the best he could.

Then he'd work on finding a place for them to live until Drea's house was available.

After this morning, he knew he couldn't continue sharing a room with Drea and stick to the terms of their arrangement.

He smelled the antiseptic air of the hospital, but remembered her sweet scent. They needed a place like they'd had in Kuwait—at least two bedrooms, two baths. That way he'd only had to see her when they ate.

And he wouldn't need to fight to keep his hands off her. He wouldn't watch her as she dressed and clamp down on his desire to prevent himself from launching across the room and tumbling her into the bed. Not have to see that honey-sweet skin that drew him like a magnet, not have to remember long silky legs, shiny satiny hair.

Celibacy was a killer. It'd been more than two years since he'd slept with a woman. That must be why he was reacting this way.

Once they were established in their own place, with separate bedrooms and their old routine, he'd be fine. He'd managed this past year without touching her, without watching every move she made, without craving her. He could resume their semblance of normalcy as soon as they found a place of their own.

He pushed away from the wall and started back to the waiting room. He paused in the doorway, his gaze drawn instantly to Drea. She was laughing at something Becky said. For a moment a deep longing pushed up from the very heart of him.

She'd often smiled at him over the past decade. But it'd

always been a polite smile, never loving and open like the ones she shared with Becky. Her entire face was lit with amusement and love for his sister. Her dark eyes sparkled and shimmered in humor.

Keith stepped into the room wanting that warmth and shared humor directed at him. But when she saw him, her face froze, then the polite mask he knew so well dropped into place.

"Ready to leave?" Drea asked as she rose.

"Yes. I want to run by the construction site. We'll come back tonight. Dad's waiting for you, Becky. Mom went to the business office to finalize a few things. She'll be back in a little while. I think he'll sleep the rest of the day. The doctor's going to be here tonight so we'll get all our answers then."

Becky bade them both a cheery goodbye and went to take her turn visiting her dad.

In only moments Keith and Drea were in the car.

"I'll drop you off at the house before I head for the construction site."

"So your dad asked you to take over," she confirmed.

"Yes, just as you predicted. Not that it changes anything with us."

She clenched her teeth. "Do you really think I'm such a mercenary? That now that you'll have a company to run I'll expect lavish amounts of money? That I expect you to set me up in some sort of fancy style? I told you before I don't need any money."

He shrugged. "Just making sure you know the rules didn't change."

"Stop comparing me to Diane. I'm not like her. I don't have a gambling problem. I'm not lying to you about any debts I've run up. And I certainly don't have a lover on the side."

"What about your declaration this morning about finding another man?"

She tilted her head and watched him, trying to figure out exactly why he seemed angry.

You don't need another man, I'm man enough for you. You're mine and I'm not letting you go.

She watched for endless minutes, but his lips remained firmly pressed together, thinned with anger.

Okay, so he wasn't going to say that, but she wouldn't let him get away with what he had said.

"You know I meant after the annulment. When I'm single I'd like to meet up with someone. Do you want me to remain alone the rest of my life?"

He was silent, hearing her words echo in his mind.

Alone the rest of her life?

No, he couldn't ask that. Couldn't expect that. She was young, only twenty-seven. She had her whole life before her.

Because she helped him out when he needed it this past year was no reason to expect her to devote herself to his memory once they went their separate ways.

Alone the rest of her life.

He was going to be alone the rest of his. What was the big deal?

At least that way there'd be no one to steal his money, no one to trash his heart. He'd be in control of every aspect. He'd be content to work and hang out with friends. Marriage wasn't for him.

He remembered her saying she liked being part of a couple.

If he were honest, he'd admit he'd enjoyed the past year. Company events had been tolerable with her at his side. Thinking it over, he believed he got the better part of their deal. But she'd never once complained.

"I know you got a raw deal with Diane, but I'm not her and I don't want to keep getting her backwash. I'll stay with you until your dad's better, then I'm finding someone who'll want to build a future together. After seeing pictures of Tyler and Trevor and hearing Becky talk, I want children more than ever. I think I want at least three. I'm all alone in the world, Keith. I need a family to love."

He was silent the rest of the way to his parent's house. He couldn't argue with her. But he didn't have to like it.

When he pulled into the driveway, he looked at her.

"I'm heading for the work site. I don't know when I'll be home. In time to go back to the hospital for sure."

"That's fine. I'll unpack the rest of my things and iron what needs ironing. I'll fix something for dinner. Do you think you can make it by six?"

Waiting only for his nod, Drea exited the car hurried toward the steps, not wanting to even think. She needed to find a way to get this man to change his mind about her or find it in herself to get over him and get on with her life.

Becky brought Peggy Branson home soon after. Not able to stay, Becky again invited Drea and Keith to dinner later in the week and then kissed her mother goodbye.

"They're planning to operate tomorrow," Peggy said sadly as she trailed Drea into the kitchen.

"Let me fix you a cup of tea," Drea said. "Sit down and rest, you need to keep your strength up for Matt."

She bustled about the familiar kitchen fixing her mother-in-law a hot cup of tea, chatting with her as she tried to take her mind off the seriousness of her husband's illness and the uncertainty of the operation.

"I'm so glad you and Keith came home, Drea. Becky's so busy with the boys and Tom and with being pregnant. I don't want her worrying too much. But I've needed someone. You know I've always depended on Matt. Maybe too much. I don't know what I'll do if he doesn't recover."

"He'll be fine, you have to hold on to that thought. He's getting the best care possible and has one of the finest doctors in Virginia. You were such a help to me when Daddy was so sick, I'm glad I can be here for you."

Peggy nodded, taking a sip of tea, her eyes flooding with tears.

"I was sorry your father died when he did. It gave us all a jolt of realization of our own mortality. Maybe that's what Keith needed to propose to you. At least that's one less thing I have to worry about—Keith's happiness."

Drea smiled, hoping the expression on her face looked happy.

Her heart ached for the woman and her pain. At least for the time being she and Keith could keep the knowledge from his parents that they wouldn't be living happily ever after. He'd been right to ask her to stay until his father recovered.

She'd do her part to the bitter end.

Settling Peggy down to rest, Drea wandered around the house, finally moving to the big swing that hung from one of the old oak trees in the backyard. It reminded her of the swing at her own home.

She had yet to notify the realty company that it was time to give notice to her tenants.

She brought her notepad to check off some of the items on her list and began to make a new one. First, new clothes, something with a little more oomph than what she normally wore. If the fancy underwear didn't work to catch Keith's attention, maybe she'd try something a little more blatant.

Then there was her hair. Should she get it cut? She'd ask Becky.

How about makeup? And provocative moves? Those she needed to practice. She wasn't used to flirting. Was that a learned trait? She sure hoped so.

Swinging back and forth in the dappled shade, she gazed off into space. Maybe she should run by the library. She could visit with her old colleagues and check out any books she could find on flirting.

She remembered the old checking account she'd shared with her father. She needed to check its balance, check the signature card. She jotted a note. She ask Peggy if she could take on the cooking while she and Keith stayed there. It'd help out her mother-in-law and give her something to do.

She could also fix Keith's favorite meals. She'd carefully taken notes when he complimented her on the meals in Kuwait and knew what he liked best. The way to a man's heart...

Drat, she needed to check if there were any other investments of her dad's.

The list was becoming a mishmash of different topics. She leaned back in the swing and let her imagination soar, imagining herself with Keith.

Late that afternoon Keith pulled into the driveway bone tired. He'd reviewed the standings at the two sites in progress, spent time in Branson Construction's small office focusing on the financial statements.

The business was in trouble. His father hadn't been working up to capacity for months. There were labor problems, material shortages and bills in arrears. One site was in danger of losing its financial backing.

Just what he needed—a troubled company to deal with, in addition to everything else.

Why had his dad let things slide? Had his health been bad for so long? Why hadn't he said something earlier?

Sighing softly, he climbed out of the car and headed into the house. Opening the door, Keith paused a moment taking a deep breath of the tantalizing aroma. He walked to the kitchen where Drea and his mother worked together preparing the meal.

They'd all go back to the hospital in another hour or so and again tomorrow for the surgery. He was tired and depressed but wanted to hide it from everyone.

"Keith!"

Drea spun around when she heard him and smiled in warm welcome. Taking three small steps, she flung herself against his chest and reached up with her arms to pull his head down to kiss him.

Instinctively Keith wrapped his arms around her and returned the kiss. He felt warmth and softness, smelled sweetness and innocence, tasted hunger and desire. The mouth-watering aromas of ham and sweet potatoes baking in the oven mingled with the light flowery fragrance that was Drea's own.

Her mouth welcomed his in a kiss so distracting that for a split second he forgot where he was. He could only feel the armful of soft femininity that enveloped him.

Pulling back slightly, Drea looked at him with warning, rolling her eyes toward his mother.

A pretense. He should have known.

"How was your day?"

Slowly she released him, even more slowly pushed away as his arms reluctantly opened.

He appreciated her keeping up their pretense in front of his mother. He could play at this, too.

"Hectic. Trouble at both sites, a ton of paperwork waiting at the office."

His mother hurried over, her face wrinkled in worry.

"Is it bad? I had a feeling things weren't going well. But you know your father, he never brought work home with him. Can you fix it?"

"Of course I will, Mom." He brushed a kiss against her cheek. "The cavalry arrived just in time. You don't need to worry, I'll turn things around in a few weeks. Dinner smells wonderful. How long before we eat?"

"Another twenty minutes. If you want to take a quick shower, there's time," Drea said as she turned back to the biscuit dough she'd been rolling, remembering his routine from Kuwait.

Her insides felt squishy from his kiss. She knew he was stunned at her flinging herself against him, but she planned to do all she could to maintain their charade before his mother. She couldn't let Peggy suspect everything wasn't perfect in her son's marriage.

Drea would need to explain to Keith, though, so he didn't think she'd lost her mind.

"A shower is just what I need." He ran his fingers through his hair as he started for the hall bathroom.

Stripping off his clothes once in the bathroom, he ran the water hot and stepped beneath the spray. For a second he could feel the impression of Drea's body against his. In the steamy bathroom he could still smell the sweet scent of her. Every time he brushed past her, he'd smell the soft scent that was Drea's own. Blindfolded, he could find her by her own special fragrance.

The feel of her in his arms aroused him. Reaching out, he shut off the hot water and stood beneath the cold spray. He had too much to worry about with his father's surgery, his mother's concerns and now the problems at the construction sites.

He didn't need a complication in the form of some unmanageable attraction for Drea. Something had to be done, and fast, to regain the distance they'd maintained in Kuwait.

They needed their own place!

Keith dressed in clean jeans and a soft cotton shirt. When he joined his mother and Drea in the kitchen, they were setting the table. He helped—anything to keep his eyes off Drea.

When they sat to eat, his mother placed him opposite his wife. Keith studied her as she talked easily with his mom, keeping the conversation firmly upbeat and on happy topics.

They discussed the rose show held a few weeks back and the prize his mother won for her heritage roses.

Drea asked if his mother had heard anything about her tenants. The Bransons had been named as contacts while she and Keith were in Kuwait.

Her voice was soft and sweet, a husky alto that sent tendrils of awareness through him. Keith liked listening to her. He'd known her for years, yet never before appreciated how sexy her voice sounded.

What would it be like in the dark, whispering words of love?

Scowling at his wayward thoughts, he tried to focus on the conversation. Realizing both women were staring at him, he blinked.

"What?"

"I asked what was wrong at the company," his mother said gently.

"Just needs Dad's hand. I'll step in until he's better," Keith said.

"If he gets better." His mother's eyes filled with tears.

"He will," Keith stated firmly.

"Even if he does, the company's grown too large for one man to run," Peggy said.

"Nonsense, Dad's done it for years."

"But he's not as young as he used to be."

"He'll be fine, Mom."

"And he'll recover so much faster knowing Keith's in charge while he's gone," Drea added, reaching out to grasp the older woman's hand in comfort. "That's one less worry Matt will have. He can concentrate on getting well."

"Maybe Matt should retire," Peggy said hesitantly.

Drea nodded.

"If he wants he could consider that option. I'm sure Keith would take over the business. Wouldn't you?" She turned her dark eyes on him.

He stared at her, trying to discern what convoluted thoughts spun in her mind. Why was she pushing him so hard to take over his father's business?

Did she plan to hang on and make the most of the turn of events?

Branson Construction had been a well-run, profitable company before he left for Kuwait. It'd easily turn around, if it had some focused management. He could do it and she knew it.

"I'll run it as long as Dad needs me," he said slowly, wanting once again to make sure Drea knew he hadn't changed their agreement. He'd make sure she knew there was never going to be a repeat of history.

This time his wife wouldn't take all his money and move on to greener pastures.

Chapter Seven

Drea smiled slowly as she watched Keith's suspicious gaze. She knew exactly what he was thinking, trying to figure out how she planned to hurt him the way Diane had.

Well, he was in for a surprise. She had no intention of hurting him. She loved him. She only wanted to be able to prove that to him.

Keith needed the responsibility of Branson Construction. If they joined forces, his dad would give him an important role in the company.

And that vote of confidence would go a long way to making life easier for the tough, bitter man who thought his world had ended a couple of years ago.

She knew from Becky's emails that his father was thinking of retiring. Maybe because of his illness or maybe because of his age but Matt wanted to take time to enjoy life with his wife. Maybe do some traveling after he turn over the day-to-day operations to his son.

Keith needed to stop being suspicious of everyone and everything. It was time he took the blessings life offered him and made the most of them.

"We should be going to the hospital soon," Peggy said,

unaware of the rising tension between them.

"Maybe Drea should stay home," Keith said, frowning at her.

"Why?"

Startled, she stared at him. She'd planned to go tonight with everyone else. Was he already trying to wean her away from his life?

The stress is too much for you, darling. I need you strong for me. To help me make it through this hard time.

"You look tired. I know the flight home was a killer. We won't be there that long. Dad can see you after the operation. We're going primarily to meet with the doctor, pop in to see Dad, then come home. Come if you like, but I thought you might wish for an early night."

Unexpectedly Drea felt cherished. It had been a long time since anyone had taken care of her.

It wouldn't be hard to stay home. She was tired and dreaded going back to the hospital which brought back such sad memories of when her own father had been so ill.

"I could clean up here and get to bed early," she said slowly.

"Keith's right. I should have thought of it. Get a good night's rest. Tomorrow will be so stressful until we know the results of the surgery," Peggy said, concern in her every gesture.

"Drea doesn't have to go tomorrow, either. I know how hard it must be for her to be at the hospital. According to the surgeon's earlier comments, the operation will take hours.

Then Dad'll spend time in the recovery room before anyone can see him."

"Oh, but—" his mother started to protest.

"I'll go tomorrow," Drea said. "I'll be there with you, Peggy."

"Are you sure?" he asked.

She nodded. "I want to be there."

She'd hate it. She'd live in fear until they knew the outcome. She hoped so desperately that Keith's father recovered, that he wouldn't lose his dad as she had.

It'd be hard, but she wanted to do it. She needed to show her husband she could be counted on in every way.

"It will be a long day," he warned.

Drea nodded.

She remembered the nightmare of her father's illness. So many hours when she sat beside his bed, willing him to live, praying for his recovery. The endless minutes when he never knew she was there.

In the end it hadn't mattered. He'd died peacefully in his sleep in the wee hours.

"I'll take some knitting, something to help pass the time."

Peggy was resolute, knowing her husband's life was on the line.

"We'll be there first thing in the morning. Becky and Tom are coming, too, aren't they?" Keith asked.

His mother nodded, smiling sadly. Everyone knew the fear she faced.

Drea blinked back tears and tried not to imagine herself

in a similar situation.

What if it were Keith whose life hung in the balance? What if she didn't know for sure whether he'd be there with her tomorrow night?

The anguish pierced her. She couldn't stand it. Even if she was unable to change his mind about marriage, she had the consolation of knowing he'd be alive and well somewhere in the world.

She glanced at him, meeting his fierce stare, hoping her expression gave nothing away.

"We'll be back before nine. Go to bed, honey, you look exhausted," he said gruffly.

He didn't like tears in Drea's eyes. It reminded him of the night he'd found her on her back porch. He hadn't liked it then and he disliked it now.

He wanted to see her smile, laugh, like she had with Becky this afternoon.

He wanted her to smile at him like that, just once.

Keith awoke the next morning with an armful of sweet, warm femininity. Drea lay sprawled all over him snuggling against his rib cage, her silky hair spread across his chest and shoulder like a blanket, one warm arm encircling him. Both of his arms surrounded her. She was fast asleep.

Instantly Keith became totally awake. Lying still, he felt the soft brush of her moist breath caress his chest as she breathed in and out. He felt the steady slow beat of her heart against his ribs. His T-shirt offered scant covering for her tantalizing body. What was she doing sprawled all over him while sleeping? The queen-size bed should be plenty big enough for the two of them to sleep without touching.

They needed to find another place to stay. Today if possible. He couldn't take much more of this without doing something they'd both probably regret.

Perspiration broke out on his forehead as he sought to control the sudden reaction to her closeness. His own heart rate sped up. She was tempting. Her curves cried out for caresses. Her hair begged him to tangle his fingertips in it and feel the silky thickness, the gentle ripple of waves. Her lips tantalized him, tempting him to cover them with his own and lose himself in her soft feminine beauty.

Struggling with temptation as old and strong as time, he did nothing. He remained perfectly still, yet absorbed every aspect of their compromising situation. When she awoke she'd probably start screaming.

This had definitely not been part of their bargain. He'd promised a platonic relationship, nothing more.

Why had his mother bought this blasted bed? In the bunk beds he'd had since childhood, they'd never have ended up like this. It'd have been easy to maintain their platonic relationship with the two separate beds.

Now he didn't know if he could open his arms and release her.

He should move away. She was still asleep; she'd never know. He should slip out from the bed and head for the shower. Another cold one.

That's what he should do.

That's exactly what he would do in just another minute.

But for one more minute he'd savor the delectable

sensations of holding Drea in his arms. Treasure the passion that rioted through him as he became minutely attuned to her sweet scent enveloping him in a haze of awareness.

He wanted to kiss her, taste the honey sweetness that he tasted last night when he'd come home from work. He wanted to caress her silky skin, touch every inch of her, learn all her secrets.

Almost shaking with the effort it cost him to remain still, he let his imagination take flight, soaring with the thrill of making love with Drea.

He hadn't been totally oblivious to her over the past year. It'd surprised him once or twice, a fleeting, compelling thought of making love with his wife.

But he remembered Diane and the risk of another debacle had been too much for him to act on. He didn't want to get tangled up in any kind of relationship that'd leave him as vulnerable as the last one had.

The rapid heartbeat beneath her right ear thrummed. Blinking slowly, Drea stretched like a boneless cat. Suddenly she became aware of exactly where she was lying, pressed up against a most decidedly male body. Stunned, she raised her head and met Keith's amused gaze.

"Awake?" he asked, his arms still holding her.

Awake and extremely aware of her proximity to Keith. Her brown eyes widened in shock and for a moment she couldn't move.

"What are you doing on my side?" she said, stacking her hands on his chest and gazing at him after glancing around the bed. Her skin tingled where he touched her. Slowly she met his gaze, holding it, wondering what he saw as he looked at her.

"Your side? Since when did we divvy up the bed?"

He liked the way she appeared flustered, confused, yet kept striving for control. Usually more reserved, the change charmed him.

"Well, this is the side I climbed into last night. Alone, I might add. And I notice you're very much on it now," she defended, meeting his gaze bravely.

He gave a lazy grin. "Maybe I want this side."

"Well, you should have said something before last night."

She shifted slightly, moving to get to the far side. She grew instantly aware of her T-shirt riding up by her waist. He felt like a furnace beneath her.

"Here I was, calmly sleeping on my back and you climbed all over me. You can't blame me for this."

She dropped her head against his shoulder, unable to face him at the moment. For a long second there was silence. She wanted to melt away so she never had to endure the embarrassment that facing him would produce.

"Why don't you slip off that silly T-shirt and kiss me, let me make love to you? We've both wanted this for so long, Drea."

She longed for the words. For once couldn't he read her mind?

"Drea, I think we need to talk about this," Keith said reasonably.

She slipped over to the other side and scrambled to her feet beside the bed.

"Talk about what?"

She backed away from temptation, yanking down the T-shirt while she tried to bring some rational thought process to bear. He was probably as embarrassed as she. And he was right, he'd done nothing. She'd been the one on top of him.

"Talk about this and why you kissed me last night."

Keith sat up in bed, fluffed up a couple of pillows and leaned back against the headboard. The sheet fell to his waist his bare chest a tantalizing distraction.

Drea resolutely kept her eyes on his.

"I kissed you last evening to reassure your mother that our marriage is normal. She mentioned how relieved she was not to have to worry about your happiness anymore. Wasn't that your reason for continuing this charade now that we're back in the States? To reassure your folks until your father's better able to handle things?"

Where was a robe when she needed it? They'd packed too hastily in Kuwait. She needed more clothes.

"I wondered if that was your reason as well, that's all. Especially in light of waking up with you all over me."

The humor appealed to him. He chuckled softly.

"It's not funny. You stay on your side of the bed." Or I'll lose what little control I have around you.

How had she ever thought she could seduce the man? He hadn't payed any attention to her in all the years he'd known her. Why did she think she had a chance in the few weeks until his father recovered? She'd practically been naked in his arms this morning and he was laughing.

And she'd panicked.

He snapped back the sheets in a sudden move and stalked over to her. Drea stared at him. He was overwhelmingly masculine! She couldn't keep her eyes from tracking down his chest to his white briefs, down his long muscular legs, back up to his wide tanned chest.

Fire scorched her cheeks and she jerked her gaze up to meet his. Humor had fled. Something else, dark and steady, replaced it.

In two steps he crowded against her, drawing her into his arms, his mouth descending slowly, giving her time to protest. Then he kissed her.

The shock of the kiss held Drea immobile. Then feelings like she'd never known overtook her. Heat curled deep within as shimmering waves of desire flooded her, rendering her legs weak, her hands incapable of pushing him away, as the small part of sanity that remained urged her to do.

When his lips moved against hers, Drea responded. She ignored the warning signals emitted from her brain and gave way to the passion enveloping her. For long moments she reveled in the exquisite sensations shimmering through her.

Time was forgotten. The bedroom became a cloud, the sunshine in the window exploded into rainbows of pleasure as she floated on pure delight.

Chapter Eight

"Keith?" Peggy Branson knocked on the door. "Keith, are you awake? You have a long-distance call from Markham International."

"Be right there, Mom," he called in response.

His eyes glittered down into Drea's as his hands slowly unwound from her hair.

"I need to take the call," he said as he turned swiftly and drew on his jeans, zipping them as he headed out the door.

Drea stood absolutely still, stunned. Her heart rate was frantic. She took a deep breath. She'd been hoping to seduce him with some indication of affection. Was that amazing kiss the first step? Would it lead to something more?

She couldn't believe how she felt from a kiss.

Grabbing her clothes, she headed for the bathroom. Moments later she turned on the shower, stripped off his T-shirt and stepped beneath the soothing spray.

What had happened? Sighing with disappointment that his mother had interrupted she wondered if her goal was hopeless. She wanted some show of affection, an indication that she meant something him. She knew he didn't love her. He might never trust another woman again after the mess of his first marriage. But she'd hoped for the closeness of friendship. Was that too much to ask?

Instead she felt as if he'd kissed her in answer to an unvoiced request from her. She no longer felt cherished as she had last night when he suggested she stay home. She wasn't sure what to expect in the next few weeks.

But if that kiss was anything to go by, he definitely wasn't repulsed by her.

And wasn't that what she wanted? For him to see her as an available, desirable woman? One who'd relish being in his arms, delight in sharing their lives.

And one who would enjoy nights with him beyond anything she'd known.

Yet without affection, without love, was there any possibility of a future together? Could she draw closer physically and then walk away heart-whole in a few weeks?

Keith dragged his fingers through his hair as he hurried down the stairs to the kitchen. Giving his mother a quick kiss on the cheek in passing, he snatched up the phone, but his thoughts remained with Drea.

What had come over him?

She'd seemed embarrassed when she flounced off the bed. From the way she reacted to his kisses, she wasn't totally averse to him. Who'd have expected his shy, somewhat prim little wife to kiss so explosively?

It made him wonder again what she'd be like in bed. Obviously she wouldn't be the same quiet woman he'd spent the past year with. If her kisses were an indication, she'd be a fireball—honey-hot and sweet.

"Branson here," he said into the receiver. Listening for a moment, he frowned. "No way to expedite?"

Just what he needed, another problem. The fact that their belongings were being held up and probably wouldn't arrive for another six weeks would concern Drea as well.

He hung up impatiently when the call was finished, turned to head back to the bedroom. Couldn't one thing work out smoothly?

"We need to leave soon," his mother said gently from across the kitchen. She looked older today, frightened.

"We'll be down in plenty of time, Mom," Keith said gently, going across to give her a hug. He gave her a quick kiss, anxious to get back upstairs.

Once he reached the top of the stairs, he heard the shower.

"Drea, you going to hog the bathroom all morning?" Keith banged on the closed door a half hour later. He'd come back to their room hoping to resume where they'd left off and found her ensconced in the bath.

Frustrated, he paced the narrow space between the bed and the wall. Finally giving in to his impatience, he'd moved to the hall, knocking on the door.

"I'm almost ready," she called.

Gazing at her reflection in the mirror, Drea took a deep breath, tried to quiet the roiling nerves that gave her no rest. She had to face him again. There was no way she could spend the rest of her life in the bathroom.

But what would she say?

And what if he kissed her again? She'd never be able to

resist, that much she knew. And why should she? They were married. Maybe it'd show him they belonged together.

Yeah, right.

Taking a deep breath, she turned and opened the door. And almost walked right into the solid wall of his chest.

"Oh." Startled, she glanced up.

Keith stared down at her with an intense gaze. Slowly he reached out and wrapped a tendril of her still damp hair around one finger, anchoring her in place as surely as if he'd poured cement around her.

She dropped her gaze to his broad chest and her longings rose. Daringly she let one hand drift up and permitted her fingertips to brush against the muscles that stretched beneath his tanned skin.

She heard him draw in his breath and immediately met his heated gaze. The reckless abandonment of old habits surprised her. Slowly she took a deep breath and smiled.

"Mom's worried we won't get to the hospital in time," he said, his thumb rubbing over the silky strand of hair twirled around his fingers.

I didn't mean to be so long, she said, her voice husky with emotion. "Was the call important?" Important enough to interrupt us?

"You could say that. There's been a snafu with shipping our personal things. They won't be here for another six weeks."

"Six weeks!"

Gone were the amorous feelings coursing through her as the impact of what he told her hit hard.

"Keith, I'm right in the midst of revisions. I need my computer. I can't wait another week, much less six."

"We'll get you one. You kept your backup in the cloud, didn't you?"

"Yes."

The momentary panic eased.

Things were happening too fast. Keeping a tight rein on her control proved harder than anything. She'd longed for some physical contact with him for so long she couldn't resist when he offered, no matter what the reasons.

Stepping closer, she skimmed her hand up his chest to his shoulder, around the nape of his neck, brushing against the thick hair that grew a little long. Daringly Drea stepped even closer.

His fingers threaded into her hair and he lowered his mouth to gently touch her parted lips. The explosive reaction to that light touch startled her. She was again surprised to find the feelings so intense. Giving in to the invitation, she gently relished all the delights of their kiss.

"You pack a wallop, lady," he said, drawing back as he heard his mother moving downstairs.

Drea snapped back to reality.

They were out in the open in the hallway. Keith still needed to get dressed and get his mother to the hospital before eight.

"You're not so bad yourself," she said, smiling shyly.

Reluctantly bringing her hands down, she stepped around him and headed toward their room. "The bathroom's all yours."

As Keith drove swiftly to the hospital all Drea could think of was their kiss. She'd insisted on sitting in the back letting Peggy sit in front beside her son. Drea hoped the distance would give her some calming perspective, but she couldn't find any watching his every move.

She loved the way he looked, his sun-bleached hair that definitely needed a trim soon, his angular jaw so confidently set as he faced the day's challenges. Loved his understated strength that radiated in all situations. It wasn't only physical strength from working in construction, but the strength of determination and purpose that sat so well in him. Even the blow of losing so much because of Diane hadn't slowed him down.

Drea began to consider whether she ought to regroup, to hold off on her nebulous plan to see exactly what Keith might offer.

She started to believe she should take what she could get and let the dreams of love and affection simmer.

Maybe he'd grow to love her. Maybe he'd enjoy real affection enough that he'd want to stay married.

Would that be enough for her?

Would marriage without Keith's love be preferable to life alone?

Becky and Tom were already waiting at the hospital. So began an endless day. There was nothing to do but wait while the surgeon used his skill to save the life of Matt Branson.

Peggy brought her knitting. Becky and Drea talked, walked on the lawn, returned to eat a scant lunch at the hospital cafeteria.

Finally, just after two, the surgeon came to tell them the operation had been a success.

"He's in recovery now. You can peek in on him, one at a time. But he won't know you're there. In fact, it'll be tomorrow morning before he's fully awake and aware again. I suggest you see him now and then return later or even wait until tomorrow. He's going to be fine."

Peggy had tears running down her cheeks. Becky turned to Tom and he enfolded her in his arms.

Drea blinked back tears of relief, startled when Keith put his arm around her shoulders and hugged her gently.

"You doing okay?" he whispered.

She nodded. "I'm so glad he's going to be okay. How are you doing?"

"I'm feeling a whole lot better than I have since we got the call."

Peggy wanted to stay to see her husband, stay in the room with him even if he didn't know she was there.

Keith, confident his father was on the road to recovery, was anxious to get to the construction site and get busy working to save the company.

He invited Drea to go with him, to see if there was extra computer.

Once he was sure his mother was set, they left.

The Windmere project site was hot and dusty. The earth had been graded and smoothed in preparation for the houses that already had foundations poured. Several lonely trees clung to the dusty ground, evidence of Matt Branson's effort to retain the mature trees where possible.

Two dozen houses stood in various stages of construction, framing up in some, plumbing already begun in others. None were enclosed as yet and Drea was intrigued to look through the wood frames at the expanses that would one day be individual rooms.

Men were everywhere, hammering nails, sawing wood, stringing electrical wire. The activity looked chaotic yet Drea knew each man was an expert at his job and the homes were going up efficiently.

Keith unlocked the construction trailer and threw open the door. Peering inside curiously, Drea paused for a moment while he flicked on the air conditioner. The trailer was stifling. They'd need the cooling system operating on high to keep it manageable in the hot Virginia summer.

There were two desks, an assortment of filing cabinets and a drafting table with blueprints and schematics scattered across it. The desks were piled high with stacks of papers, permits and invoices, notes of modifications and sales literature.

"You can use that desk today, that computer. Just dump the stuff from the desk onto mine. I have to go through everything to get a handle on what's going on," Keith said, turning to flip on the answering machine.

As the messages played, Drea walked over to the desk indicated and began to gather up the stacks of papers. She placed them on the edge of Keith's desk, noticing how close the desks were. She wouldn't have the luxury of being on her own in a quiet room to create. She'd be in the middle of a working construction site with the boss man right beside her.

A very disturbing boss man, at that.

She sat at the computer, pleased to discover it was the same model as the one she had. Now, she thought as she pressed the on button, if it only had the same software she used, she'd be back in business. When the main menu came up, she was pleased to see it did. Waiting while the computer fully booted up, she studied Keith sitting only a half-dozen feet away, his eyes catching hers.

She wrinkled her nose at him. "Don't you have to take notes on those calls?

He paused the answering machine and grinned at her. "So far I can remember everything. A man likes a pretty view."

She turned back to the computer, the unexpected compliment flooding her with pleasure. She wasn't sure what to do. She wasn't sure she could write with distraction so close.

Drea accessed her account on the cloud and opened up the first chapter of her latest book to catch up the story line. Her editor liked the manuscript, liked the continuing main character and was impatiently awaiting revisions. Drea was ahead of schedule. If she completed it early, her publisher had promised they would bump her up in the release schedule.

Men came and went, discussing needs and plans with Keith. Each time one showed up, she was distracted. She watched Keith talk to the different men, go over blueprints and delivery schedules.

She noticed how he kept his impatience under control, how quickly he identified potential problems and offer solutions.

When he left the trailer to show one man what he wanted

a blast of hot air infiltrated the trailer. He shrugged out of his shirt, wearing only a white T-shirt that matched the one she used as a nightie.

Drea gave up all pretense of writing and went to the window. Keith picked up a tool belt and strapped it on. She smiled. It reminded her of an old-fashioned gunslinger. The belt hung on his slim hips, riding low. The jeans were snug, displaying the long length of his muscular legs.

He plopped on the hard hat and turned unexpectedly, his gaze connecting with hers through the dusty glass. Drea stared back, fascinated. Caught up in the heat of his eyes, she couldn't move. Then he smiled slowly and turned back to the construction worker at his side.

"Think you're so smart to catch me out, don't you?" she murmured. "But I caught you out, too, Mr. Know-it-all."

It was only when she saw Keith heading back toward the trailer that she dashed over to the computer and began to read what was on the monitor.

She focused on her plot, the clues she hoped weren't too obvious, the characterization, delving more and more into the reasons and motives of the protagonists, trying to build suspense as the hero faced danger again and again.

When had her hero begun to resemble Keith? When had the female in this book begun to resemble herself? She flicked a quick glance up as Keith strode into the trailer.

"Miss me?" he teased.

"Oh, were you gone?"

Chuckling, he tossed aside the belt and hat and confidently crossed the trailer and leaned over her, resting his hands on the arms of her chair.

"As if I didn't see you in the window."

"Why were you looking?"

"Just to see what I saw."

Drea grew more and more aware of him as the silence lengthened. She rested her hands on his hot arms, clutching for sanity's sake.

"This isn't a good idea," she said breathlessly, wishing with all her heart he'd kiss her again.

"What isn't?"

His voice was like hot wine, intoxicating every nerve ending as his eyes never left hers.

"Trying to work here."

She loved seeing this side of Keith, but so far she'd hardly accomplished any work. At this rate she wouldn't be finished before Christmas.

His breath brushed across her cheeks. Suddenly her lips tingled. She wished he'd kiss her like he had that morning, hot and passionately. She liked the way she felt when he kissed her, the way her body tingled and responded. Was it like an addiction? The more she had, the more she'd crave?

She slid her hands up his arms, across his shoulders and to his neck, tugging experimentally. Keith gave a half smile and lowered his head to her urging.

She was ready when he kissed her. Drawing her to her feet, he wrapped his arms around her and molded her body to his. Drea felt surrounded by his heat.

Chapter Nine

"Say, Keith—Oops, bad timing."

The door slammed shut.

Drea pulled back, horrified.

"It was one of the men," she exclaimed.

"Sounded like it."

Keith turned and headed out the door.

Drea sank back down on her chair. There was no way she was going to get any work done here. They'd more than proved that.

And she didn't want Keith's authority undermined by any hanky-panky on-site with his wife. She'd see if she could take the computer home and work there.

She needed privacy to be able to concentrate on her book. It was too easy to look up and let her gaze feast on the sexy image her husband projected.

Keith didn't return for almost a half hour. When he did, Drea was ready to leave.

"I called the hospital. Your mom's gone home. Your dad's doing as expected, still asleep. I'm ready to go home when you are. Can I take the computer? Working here isn't an option."

She used her best librarian voice. She refused to meet his

eyes, but focused on his chin. She didn't want to get distracted before they got home.

"Yes to going home, yes to taking the computer. I guess working here was a bad idea. I couldn't concentrate."

Drea looked up at that. So she hadn't been the only one affected.

It made her feel hopeful about the future.

"Tell me about the book you're working on," Keith invited as he drove away from the building site.

It occurred to him he'd never really asked about her work. He'd been too distracted and furious at Diane at the beginning of their marriage to think of anything else.

They'd fallen into a pattern of working and eating and sleeping in Kuwait that had excluded much conversation between them.

Gradually his anger toward Diane had faded. The anger at himself for being so oblivious had gradually eased.

But he'd never thought to ask Drea about her work.

She wrote every day and he didn't know if she still liked writing or found it tedious. If she were worried about writer's block or if the words poured from her.

Had her books sold well?

They must have, her editor kept asking for more.

"It's another John Taylor book. He's the ex-CIA agent that solved the other mysteries," she said.

"You have the same hero in every book?"

She nodded. "Yes. I like him."

"Does he remind you of me? Did you pattern your hero after me? Are there any romantic elements in the book that I should look at?"

If only he'd let her write his dialogue!

"Is it easier to keep the same hero book after book?" he asked.

"As compared to what? I've only done it this way so I don't know. The challenging part is to bring John alive in every book without repeating previous books. Yet I have to give enough information that a person who didn't read earlier books can understand and know him as well as people who have read all the books in order."

"This is the third?"

Smiling gently, she shook her head. "The fifth. The third book just hit the bookstores. Book four will come out at Christmas and this one next summer if not earlier. I'm contracted to finish it by the end of next month, but I'm shooting to finish earlier."

He threw her a quick glance. "I'm sorry to say I haven't read any of them."

He was sorry. Writing was her passion. He should have taken at least a token interest in it. She'd willingly helped him out of a tight spot when he'd asked her. Many nights he'd talked to her about his work in Kuwait. She'd listened with every appearance of interest when she probably hadn't a clue to most of what he was talking about. She'd always asked about his job and he'd never reciprocated.

The least he could have done was read one of her books, talked to her a bit about her writing. Maybe spent more time with her in Kuwait.

She must have been lonely, yet she never complained. In fact, he couldn't remember ever hearing Drea complain about anything How did she stay so content?

For a moment an unexpected feeling of protectiveness took hold. He wanted to protect her from his own rude behavior, his own ignorance of her writing, from the hurt she must feel that he'd never inquired about it.

He'd known her for years; she was almost another member of his family. For that reason alone he should have shown more interest in what she was doing.

And as his wife, he certainly should have shown some interest.

"Are they good?" he asked whimsically.

He'd get a copy of one today and read it. Good or bad, he wanted to see how she wrote. Did she give away part of herself in the writing? Or was it all fiction? And why mysteries?

She was such a feminine woman, he'd have expected romance novels.

"I think they're good. And people are buying them."

"Will you make enough to live on? I know writers don't make much money, unless they're some superstar bestselling author. Will you be able to manage once we separate?"

That protectiveness reared up again. Had he made a mistake taking her from her job at the library? Would she be able to manage on her own?

"I'll manage. In fact—"

"You'd tell me, wouldn't you, if you need something, even after we're divorced?"

"I won't need anything."

"Except help in finding a husband."

He frowned. That idea appealed less and less every time

he thought about it.

"Oh, yes, except for that."

The house was closed up when they reached home. Drea went ahead to open the door. Keith followed, carrying the computer.

"Your mother went to Becky's for the evening," Drea said, reading the note Peggy had left on the counter.

"She probably didn't know when we'd be home and wanted company. I know it's been a hard day for her."

Keith walked through to the dining room and set the computer on the table. Two minutes later he placed the monitor and keyboard in place. He should get her a laptop. Easier to move around and she could write wherever she wanted.

"Should we put it there?" Drea asked from the doorway. "Won't I be in your mom's way?"

"Not as long as Dad's in the hospital. We'll eat in the kitchen, so this won't interfere. Sorry there's not a separate office for you to use."

"This'll be fine. It's what I used at home when I wrote the first book. And what I had in Kuwait."

When she returned to her house, she'd turn one bedroom into an office.

"Since Mom's not here, what do you say to our going out to dinner?" Keith asked.

She glanced up and smiled at his suggestion.

"Perfect. A date—I can get started with my lessons."

He frowned. "Not a date, just going out to dinner."

"We should treat it like a date. I haven't dated in years. I hope I haven't forgotten how," she teased.

Excitement built. She'd never gone on a date with Keith.

Would it be fun? Would he put himself out at all to make sure they had a good time or was he merely looking for a quick bite to eat before they headed back to the hospital?

"People don't forget how to date. Your whole notion about practicing to entice some man is dumb. You're fine the way you are," he said gruffly.

"Why, Keith, how nice of you to say so. Thank you."

Drea turned and glanced provocatively at him over her shoulder. "I'll just need a few minutes to change into something more suitable for dinner. Are we going dancing, too?"

"No, we're going to get something to eat, that's all."

"Okay."

"I need to shower," he grumbled, following her up the steps to the second floor.

Her hair hung down her back in a clip. He wished he could reach out and unfasten it, run the silky tresses through his fingers, rub the soft waves against his face. If she didn't stop flaunting herself, he'd forget their agreement and see if she'd like to make love.

"I knew that. You always shower as soon as you get home. I'll change while you shower and wait for you downstairs."

She grinned, thinking how this was the closest thing she had to a normal relationship with him since she'd known him.

He stormed into the bathroom. He hated cold showers, but at the rate his blood was heating, that'd be the only way to go. When he stripped and stepped beneath the water, he gasped at the shock.

He was not taking her on a date. They were just going out to have dinner. Maybe talk a little bit. She could tell him more about being a writer, about her books.

He could tell her something about what he was finding at Branson Construction.

For someone not interested in dating, he suddenly began to wonder where they'd go that was nice and would offer them a quiet dinner.

Snapping off the water, he quickly dried himself, then wiped off the mirror. He had time for a quick shave. If this were to be a date, he wanted to end it right and kiss her good-night. He didn't want his late-afternoon beard to mar her sweet satiny skin.

Not that he was *planning* to kiss her, he thought as he lathered his cheeks, though if the opportunity arose, he wanted to be ready.

Drea's kisses were hot and heady. Too potent for her to be indiscriminate with them. He have to give her some gentle pointers if she was serious about this dating business. Other men might try to take advantage of her.

An uncomfortable emotion strangely like jealousy reared up. He didn't want to think of Drea kissing other men. She was too innocent, too gentle, too sweet. She needed someone to take care of her.

Drea heard Keith begin his shower. She flung off her skirt and shirt and grabbed a dressy sundress. It was warm enough even late in the evening to wear it. Pale yellow, it had narrow straps, a fitted bodice and a flared skirt that ended just above her knees. She donned strappy white sandals.

Brushing out her hair, she sprayed a cloud of her favorite perfume and walked through it, shaking her hair so it would capture as much of the mist as possible. Then she French-braided it. A touch of makeup and she was ready. She really needed to go shopping. This dress was four years old, not at all the kind of seductive attire that'd capture Keith attention. Studying herself in the mirror, she noted her hair was neat in the braid, but hardly enticing. Would a shorter cut be more provocative?

She reached over to the notebook beside her bed, rereading some of the notations. She had left off at "flirting at every opportunity." She needed the practice, if she could convince herself to try without feeling like a total idiot.

The shower ended several minutes ago. She glanced around the room. Had Keith taken in a change of clothing or would he have to come in here to dress? Would he put on his clothes if she were still there? For a daring moment she considered plopping down on the bed and waiting for him to come in.

But she shook her head. She didn't think she was up to that.

Knocking on the bathroom door to let him know she was going downstairs, Drea was startled when it instantly opened. Keith stood in the frame, a damp towel wrapped around his waist, his face lathered for shaving.

Drea caught her breath. His shoulders gleamed in the light, tanned and damp. His chest muscles were clearly defined, firm and supple beneath his taut skin. She swallowed hard, jerking her eyes back up to meet his.

"I—" She cleared her throat. "I'll wait for you downstairs. Um, you didn't have to shave."

"I wanted to. For later."

"Later?" Her heart beat faster.

"Kisses."

"Kisses?"

She sounded like an echo.

"Kisses." Keith's gaze drifted down to her mouth.

Drea licked suddenly dry lips, her own gaze mesmerized by the gleam in Keith's. She was unable to move, unable to think, envisioning the two of them locked in a warm embrace.

"Isn't that how dates end, with a good-night kiss?" he asked softly, reaching out to capture her chin in his fingers, brushing his thumb lightly across her lower lip.

"You said kisses."

"Yes."

He smiled, his thumb brushing again.

It wasn't fair. She was about to melt under the intensity of his gaze, under the sensuous feel of his thumb. And he didn't appear the slightest bit affected.

Her heart skidded, sped up, raced. Butterflies did a salsa in her stomach. Her skin glowed with the heat that flashed through her. And her active imagination provided an image of a kiss that practically had her swooning. She could hardly wait.

"Shall we skip dinner? Let me take you to bed, darling."

"I'll be down in about ten minutes."

Keith stepped back and shut the door in her face.

Slowly Drea turned and stumbled down the stairs, holding the railing to keep from falling, half-dazed as anticipation spread.

He was planning to kiss her good-night! And not a single kiss. Kisses, he'd said.

Would the kisses lead to more?

Chapter Ten

She stopped by the mirror in the hall to check her appearance. She looked fine, hair neat, color high in her cheeks, eyes sparkling in secret delight. She danced around in a circle, already wishing the evening was over and they were started on those kisses.

Unable to sit still, Drea wandered out to the backyard to sit on the wooden swing that hung from the huge oak tree. The afternoon air was soft, warm, humid. The roses Peggy cherished were in full bloom, colorful and fragrant. Pushing back in the swing, lifting her feet as it soared forward, Drea kept her gaze on the back door. In only a few minutes her date would come out.

She was finally going on a date with Keith Branson! She'd wanted that since she was a teenager.

She didn't want to learn how to entice other men. She only wanted to be able to entice this man. She'd loved Keith for so long, somehow she thought she should instinctively be able to reach him. Yet she felt uncertain.

Was he doing this to merely humor her? Or was he serious about offering her pointers about dating? Would he calmly step aside and let her walk away, let her begin to date other men?

"You ready?" Keith called from the back door.

"Yes."

Drea sauntered across the yard to join him. He wore casual slacks and a sports jacket. She smiled at how handsome he looked. She'd be the envy of all the women at the restaurant.

"Should we write your mother a note or call her to let her know where we're going?"

"Yes, I'll call her and let her know we'll go directly to the hospital from the restaurant."

Drea waited beside him in the kitchen while he made the call. Fiddling with things on the counter, she kept her eyes on Keith, feasting on how wonderful he looked.

Time and time again her eyes rested on his firm lips. She licked her own, remembering his taste from their earlier kiss. Remembering the promise he'd implied of future kisses when the night ended. She wished he'd step up to her now and—

Keith hung up the phone and turned to her.

"Becky invited us for dinner, but I told her we already had plans. We'll go there tomorrow night, all right?"

She nodded, moving her gaze lest he guess what she'd been thinking.

"Mom called the hospital and the reports are still good on Dad. He's expected to sleep through till morning, so I don't suppose there's any need to go to the hospital tonight."

She shook her head.

"We can go eat, then swing by and pick Mom up from Becky's and bring her home when we come home."

She nodded.

"Drea, stop talking so much."

Smiling self-consciously, she met his eyes and shrugged.

Keith leaned over and brushed his lips against hers. Instantly Drea wanted more. She wanted to feel the heat from that morning. Wanted to assuage her own hunger for Keith, as if she ever could.

He lifted his head a scant inch and gazed down at her upturned face. Drea knew her expression probably showed the love that flooded her, but she couldn't help it.

"Do you want to go eat or stay here?" he asked softly, his breath mingling with hers. His lips mere millimeters from hers.

Stay here! Stay here! she wanted to scream. But she took a breath, too uncertain to give in to the urges that were almost overwhelming.

"Eat," she lied.

He nodded and straightened.

"We'll come back here," Drea said, wishing she'd answered differently. "After our date."

"We need to talk about that," he said as they headed for the car. "You want to be careful getting entangled with just anyone. Take your time. It'll take a while to get an annulment once we start the process. You shouldn't rush right out and latch on to some man."

"I've enjoyed being married, Keith," Drea said stiffly as he held her car door. "I told you, I like being part of a couple. And I want a family. If I don't want to be too old, I need to find a mate soon, don't you think?"

He slammed the door, rocking the car. She quietly

fastened her seat belt as her eyes tracked his progress around the front of the vehicle. Interesting reaction.

"Mama Celia's suit you?" he asked when he got behind the wheel.

"Sounds good."

She'd be the perfect date, agreeable and interested in what he had to say. And make it clear she was ready for a good-night kiss—and maybe more—when they got home!

Keith took them to the quiet restaurant near Waterside. They were given a small booth near the wall of windows that offered a perfect view of the marina. The sun rode low in the sky, glittering on the smooth water. The dining room wasn't crowded. The service was excellent and before long their food arrived piping hot from the kitchen.

"To your dad's speedy recovery," Drea proposed when Keith filled her wineglass.

"To Dad." He touched the rim of his to hers and then sipped.

"Can you pull the company out of its problems?" she asked as she began to eat the Maryland crab cakes she'd missed so much while in Kuwait.

"I think so. It'll take some tight management. I wish I knew why he let things slide for so long."

"You don't think it was that he lost heart when you left for Kuwait, do you?" she asked, tilting her head as she waited for his response.

It'd been something she'd wondered about. Becky's emails indicated her father's general lack of interest in things once Keith left.

Keith looked startled. "I don't think so."

She shrugged. "Just an idea. I know from Becky that your dad was very disappointed that you didn't turn to him when you had the problem with Diane."

"He offered help, but I wanted to make it on my own."

Keith didn't want to discuss the situation. It was over. He'd been a fool, but he'd learned from the event and wouldn't make the same mistake a second time.

"I'm sure he was proud of you for wanting to make it on your own, but he also wanted to help. You're his son. He hurt for you. He wanted to do something to ease your pain." Drea caught his eye. "Sometimes it's harder to take help than give it."

Keith nodded.

"Did you prove what you needed to prove?" she asked.

"That I can handle things myself?"

"Is that what you wanted to prove?"

Keith was silent so long Drea thought he wasn't going to answer. Finally he spoke.

"I felt pretty raw after Diane. I felt foolish. I should have known what she was doing, should have been able to help her stop gambling. I also should have recognized the signs she was interested in someone else. But the business needed so much attention. I didn't put the clues together."

"Usually people with problems like Diane have to want help first. And people have been betraying spouses for years. Don't let it destroy the rest of your life."

"It's not destroyed. I needed to take control of my life and find my own way out of the mess. Dad wanted me to come back into the business, but all I could see was a handout to a son who'd failed."

"I'm sure he didn't mean it that way. He wanted to help. He loves you, you're his only son. Don't you want to help him now when he needs it?"

"That's different."

Drea remained silent, watching him carefully. There wasn't much difference in the two situations, but if Keith felt better about it the way it was, she wouldn't interfere.

"It worked out, Drea. Thanks to you. I was able to pay off the rest of the debt and still have a few thousand dollars in the bank. Not enough to get started again, but I'm a lot closer."

"Maybe you should buy into your dad's business. Maybe you two could reach a compromise about what you want to build and what he wants and complement each other, rather than clash all the time," she suggested softly.

He nodded. "Maybe. It's funny you said that. It's something I've been thinking about the past couple of days. Maybe we could make it work this time."

His eyes caught her gaze and held it. Drea shivered as she felt the intensity. Dare she pursue it further, dare she try to get him to commit not only to trying a compromise with his father, but to continuing their marriage?

"Your dad'll be in the hospital for another week or so, then will need some extra care at home. By the time he and your mother are ready to be on their own, my house will be vacant. I spoke to the Realtor today and told him to give my tenants notice to vacate. We have a month-to-month agreement."

She held her breath. Would he still move in with her? Was he still planning to let their marriage continue until his father was fully healed?

Keith hesitated, drawing out the moment while he finished the last of the steak he'd ordered.

"Part of our agreement was that I'd support you while we were married."

"There's no need. The house is paid for, so our living expenses would be very small. It'd make it easier for you to get on your feet like we originally planned. And I'm making money on my books now, so—"

"You'll need to build up a backlog to carry you through between royalty checks. I know writers don't make much money. You need to be frugal to make sure you can support yourself once we separate."

If we separate, she thought, her gaze never leaving his.

"I'm doing all right."

"Good, that means you'll do even better down the road."

He reached for her hand, lacing his fingers with hers.

"We can coast along for a few months, see how things go. I want make sure you can support yourself. I know you'd expected to be supported for three years. You even gave up her job with that in mind. Nothing's really change in that regard. I need to make sure you are ready to be on your own before we end things."

"I'm sure your father will soon be on the mend and hearing our news won't delay his recovery. The agreement was for our time in Kuwait, which is now over."

"There's no rush."

"Not on my part. I thought on yours," she said.

"No."

Drea fiddled with her water glass. She should tell him she was doing well with her books. She felt somehow dishonest. She should let him know she no longer needed to depend on him for her livelihood.

Yet she could live with the small deception if it kept Keith from moving on.

"Dinner was delicious," she said, smiling brightly.

The soft strains of the music drifted in from the next room.

"I'm having fun on our date. It's odd, isn't it? Most people date, then marry. We married and now are dating and discussing an annulment."

"We decided not to discuss the annulment. Maybe later, when things are more settled."

When he was more ready to let her go. When he didn't think about taking her to bed and capturing that heat that flared between them whenever they touched.

"Will you dance with me before we go get your mom?" she asked.

Keith nodded and rose, reaching out to take her hand in his as he led her into the bar. The dance floor was small—only two other couples took advantage of the music. He pulled her into his embrace, settling her against his chest, encircling her with his strong arms.

Drea snuggled against him. She reached her arms up to his shoulders, one resting on the sleek muscles there, the other tangling gently with the thick hair at the back of his head. She felt him press against every inch of her, his muscular chest, strong legs. Leaning back slightly against the strong arms that held her so securely, she gazed up into his narrowed eyes.

"This is nice," she said softly. "Should I expect evenings like this with all my dates?"

A muscle jerked in his cheek as he dropped his face closer to hers.

"You're pushing your luck, lady. Dancing like this should be only with a man you know very, very well."

Lightly brushing his lips against hers, he tucked her head against his neck and dropped one hand to the swell of her hips, tightening his hold.

Almost unable to move for the shimmering sensations that swept through her, Drea smiled and leaned against Keith, grateful for the opportunity to be in his arms, if only for a dance.

The music segued from one romantic song into another, each one slower and dreamier than the previous. On and on they circled the dance floor, lost in a world of senses—touch and sway and soft music. The dim light cocooned them in a world of their own.

Keith knew they should leave. His father was in the hospital in serious condition. They had no business dancing the night way. He should pay the bill and drive them straight to Becky's to pick up his mom. He needed to get out of here and gain some perspective.

But he couldn't let go. He didn't want to end their evening. Drea felt like heaven in his arms. Her light fragrance surrounded him. The sweet seductive curves of her body enticed him. It was all he could do to control his hands and keep them on her back when he really wanted to find a dark place and give her endless kisses.

He couldn't take much more before he lost control completely. When the song ended, he took her hand and led her from the dance floor.

"Come on, we have to get Mom."

Drea blinked, the dreamy mood shattered. What happened? She could hardly think straight, her emotions and feelings had been so totally caught up in Keith's embrace, in the imagination she fed so fervently.

"It's not that late," she protested as he hurried her to the parking lot. "Just after ten."

"Mom'll be wondering where we are."

"I hope all my dates don't have to rush home to Mother," she said petulantly.

"Will you shut up about dates? You're a married woman and I'm your husband. I sure don't want to hear about dates."

Turning away lest he see her sudden smile, Drea's heart danced with unexpected happiness.

So wasn't that interesting—that it bothered him to talk about her dating in the future. That had to mean he wasn't as indifferent to her as he tried to pretend.

Afraid to say something that would spoil the evening, Drea remained silent until they reached Becky's place.

Peggy was waiting to leave. She and Drea spoke of their day while Keith drove. In no time they were back home.

Peggy immediately declared herself exhausted and

excused herself to go to bed. Drea bade her mother-in-law good-night and slowly turned to Keith.

"Is our evening over?" she asked softly.

He waited until he heard his mother's bedroom door close, then moved to draw Drea into his arms. "Do you want it to be over?"

Daringly she brushed her fingers against his smooth cheek, tracing the strong line of his jaw with her index finger.

"Actually, I thought you'd shaved in case we wanted to exchange a good-night kiss. I'd hate for that to have been done in vain."

With a soft groan he pulled her closer and covered her mouth with his. His lips were firm and hot and teased hers. Nibbling on her lower lip, his tongue licked the corner of her mouth. When Drea moved her head, he trailed kisses along her cheek, her jaw. Back to her lips, he kissed her for a long minute.

She shivered beneath his touch, yearning for more. She threaded her fingers in his hair and bracketed his face as he continued to kiss her.

Drea reveled in the pleasure she found in his arms, from his mouth.

He tasted of desire and heat and Keith. She couldn't get enough.

She felt the pounding beat of her heart, the gasping of breath as she fought for air. But she didn't want to stop, she wanted to continue in his arms forever.

Suddenly he broke the kiss and tipped her head back resting his forehead on hers.

Reluctantly Drea opened her eyes.

"Let me tell you something about dating," Keith said, breathing heavily.

His fingers moved to the back of her head, unfastened the clip that held her braid and began to release the strands.

"Nothing will drive a man crazier than hair that cries out to be released and mussed."

When the last plait had been released, he combed his fingers through the wavy mass. Again and again he lifted her hair, separating strands with his fingers, rubbing the tresses between his thumb and fingers. He took a handful and brought it around to rub against his cheek, slowly, as if savoring every glossy strand.

He never took his gaze from hers.

Drea felt desire blossom deep inside, swell and sweep through her like a blowtorch. She'd never felt anything so sexy. They were linked by the band of hair that he continued to rub against his skin, by their gazes locked together, by the clamoring heat inside that wanted more.

"So I should leave it hanging down in the future, not put it up?" she asked, mesmerized by the deep gleam in his silvery eyes.

"I didn't say that. When it hangs down it swirls around when you shake your head, crying out for a man's fist to wrap the silky length around it."

"What then, get it cut?"

"No! Don't get it cut."

"But if putting it up causes problems and letting it hang down causes problems, what should I do?"

She widened her gaze, as if hanging on his every word. Slowly she traced her lower lip with her tongue, her eyes daring him to refuse her blatant invitation.

"You have a dilemma, baby," he said real low as he ignored the dare and closed his mouth over hers again.

He drew his hands up her bare arms, to the thin straps of her dress. Slowly slipping his fingers beneath the material, he rubbed back and forth gently. She was so soft, her skin smooth and warm. He liked touching her. He wanted to touch every inch of her. He wanted Drea like he'd never wanted any other woman, not even Diane.

With that thought came jarring reality. Keith pulled back, pushing Drea away to hold at arm's length.

She looked puzzled. "Is something wrong?"

Her face was flushed, her lips rosy and slightly swollen. Her hair was tousled around her shoulders as if she'd just come from bed. She looked gorgeous.

"Nothing's wrong. Time to stop is all."

Chapter Eleven

Keith dropped his hands and turned away.
"Time to stop? Why?"

Who was he to say it was time to stop? Had he any idea how arousing his kisses were? How inflaming his touch was? Didn't he have any idea how much she wanted him?

"The next thing you know, we'll get carried away," he said slowly.

She put her hands on her hips, "What does that mean?"

"We need a chance to think things through. It's easy to get caught up in the heat of the moment. I don't want you doing something that you'll regret later. Sex between us can only complicate things."

"I'm not so sure. They seem pretty complicated to me right now."

Drea turned and ran up the steps. She wished she could slam the door behind her to let him know how angry she was, but that'd wake Peggy.

She grabbed his pillow from the bed and threw it against the door. She was so mad she could spit. She'd touched heaven tonight in his arms and he thought it complicated things.

She'd show him complicated. She'd get him so tied up in knots he wouldn't know which way was up. How dare he stop.

Unless…unless he hadn't been as caught up in the moment as she had been.

She sank onto the bed.

She didn't think that was the case. He'd seemed pretty involved to her.

But what did she know? She did not consider herself an expert on men. Her kisses, while nice, she was sure, certainly didn't drive him wild.

She closed her eyes in anguish. Was there nothing there for him to come to love?

She stood to take off her dress. Vowing to be the most loving wife he ever saw, she wouldn't leave unless he flat out told her to get lost. Otherwise she was sticking to him like glue to paper.

Slipping beneath the sheet, she turned out the light, wondering if he planned to come up to bed tonight.

Wondering what she could do that would make him see her as a possible partner for life.

She clung to the fact that he didn't seem to like the idea of dating other men. Was that a start?

Did that mean he wanted her for himself? What could she do to make him admit that?

Drea lay awake, counting the minutes. What was Keith doing? She came upstairs a half hour ago. Was he planning to come to bed tonight? He could easily sleep downstairs on the sofa. As long as he awakened before his mother, she'd never know, never suspect her son was anything but happily married.

Which he could be, if he only knew it, Drea repeated softly to herself. They'd been happy in Kuwait. Or at least content.

And she was nothing like Diane. Why couldn't he see that? Why couldn't he let himself relax and enjoy what they had between them, let himself envision a future with her? Give love a chance to grow?

The minutes slowly ticked by. She wasn't the slightest bit tired. Her body still hummed from the hot kisses they'd shared in the kitchen. She wanted more. She ached for the magic of his touch. Reaching out, she let her hand brush over the mattress where he slept. No matter how hard she tried, she couldn't imagine him there—she needed the reality of his presence.

Sighing, she turned over on her side. At this rate it'd be dawn before she slept.

Had he decided to sleep downstairs? Dare she go to find out?

Just then she heard Keith's tread on the steps. He was coming up after all. Her heart rate sped up in delicious anticipation. Holding her breath, she strained to listen. When the door opened, she closed her eyes, pretending sleep. She didn't want him to know she'd stayed awake waiting for him.

Let him think she hadn't a care in the world and that his kisses hadn't been the most wonderful thing that ever happened to her. She had a certain amount of pride, didn't she?

She heard every move he made. She knew when he shed his shirt and tossed it over the chair. She heard the rasp of his zipper and heat flushed through her as she recalled the sculpted planes of his hard, muscular body. She wished she dared turn on the light. Wished she dared let her eyes trace the golden tanned skin from his broad shoulders to his strong chest.

She breathed in and out, counting the seconds, trying desperately to keep her breathing even and deep. She gripped the sheet beneath her hand.

The bed dipped when he climbed in. The air against her skin cooled as he lifted the sheet to slide beneath it. Then he settled on his pillow.

Drea concentrated on breathing, her nerves at full alert. Her body tingled as she felt him near, felt his warmth, felt his presence fill the room.

And her yearning grew.

She almost stopped breathing when an idea flashed into her mind. It was brilliant, even if she did say so herself. Slowly she opened her eyes to determine how dark it was. Black as pitch—perfect.

With a soft sigh and slow stretch, she rolled over until she ran into Keith. Slowly she snuggled up against him, letting one leg across his, letting her arm slowly encircle his chest. She forced her breathing to remain even and hoped to goodness he couldn't feel the rapid beat of her heart. She didn't want him to know she was awake—he might reject her, feel duty-bound to push her away.

"Oh baby, you're going to be the death of me," Keith said softly, gathering her up into his arms, resting her head against his shoulder. He rested his cheek against the top of her head, his soft breath skimming her hair.

Keith had been doing some serious thinking downstairs. A year ago everything had seemed so clear-cut. He'd marry Drea, they'd go to Kuwait for three years. When they returned, they'd separate.

Now that plan was shot to bits and he couldn't seem to formulate a replacement.

She had every reason to expect him to support her for three years. That'd been the original plan. But it'd also been his intention to keep their relationship purely platonic. That had been blown away when they were forced to share a bed to keep up the pretense for his mom.

For a year he'd done his best to ignore the compelling femininity of his wife that seemed to intensify as the time went on. To be married to a woman and have to keep his distance hadn't been easy, but he'd done it. There'd been work enough to keep him occupied until he was too tired to do anything at night but sleep.

The fact that they now had to share a bed wasn't the only change.

Drea herself had changed. She'd been so circumspect in Kuwait. He almost didn't recognize her here.

Gone was the cool, collected wife who'd shared his apartment. In her place was a warm vibrant woman who looked at him with flirtatious provocation. Who responded to his kisses with ones so hot and potent he had trouble remembering his name.

Had he just wasted a year?

They needed to talk about the future.

Maybe they should continue with the original plan. If he lived with her at her home, two more years would ensure he could save enough to get back into the business, either on his own or in partnership with his father.

It'd also ensure that Drea would have a chance to build up some reserves. The last thing he wanted to do was threaten her livelihood.

But he didn't like depending on her cooperation to make it all work. He didn't like depending on anyone.

He sighed. He'd have to think about it some more.

Drea smelled the brandy on his breath which surprised her. They hadn't had spirits of any kind in Kuwait. Since returning home, they hadn't had anything beyond wine. Why the need for brandy?

Immediately following that thought, she wondered what he'd taste like now. Her hand rested on his strong chest. She wanted to trace every inch. She longed to reach up and brush her lips against him, taste him and brandy.

But she held herself still. It was torture. This definitely hadn't been one of her brighter ideas. How long could she pretend to be asleep when every nerve ending in her body craved his touch so much she almost trembled with need?

She swallowed and tried to think of something else. She'd blow the whole thing by giving in to the wanton pictures that danced in her brain—the two of them face to face, breast to chest, hip to hip, on the bed, making glorious hot love.

"Go to sleep, Drea," he said ever so softly.

She froze. He knew she was awake.

Embarrassed, she tried to push away, only to have his

arms tighten and hold her in place.

"We've slept like this the last couple of nights, we can do it again. Go to sleep." His voice was a rough, husky growl.

She tried to relax. It felt right to be in his arms. She wanted more, but for tonight she had this. He hadn't pushed her away. Slowly her heart rate returned to normal. Slowly the tension slipped away. Slowly she felt herself falling asleep.

Drea awoke the next morning nestled against Keith. Her back was against his chest, his thighs rested beneath hers. His breath brushed against her neck as he breathed deeply. Instantly aware of him as never before, she wondered what she should do.

To turn around and kiss him offered the most daring choice. She didn't think she could pull that off. But she didn't want to leave the bed until he awoke. For a little while she could cherish the feelings that rushed through her. Savor this special time with Keith.

"Awake?" he asked softly.

"Uh, huh," she muttered, turning so she could face him.

"Have you always been this pretty or is it a recent thing?" he asked, moving his gaze across her face.

She smiled her pleasure at his compliment. "What do you think?"

Was that sultry voice hers? Was she actually flirting with him?

"I think I've been blind. All these years I've only seen you as Becky's friend."

"And now?"

"And now I–"

"Keith? Are you and Drea awake? I have hotcakes ready for the griddle. I want to get to the hospital early to be there when your father wakes up," Peggy's voice called up the stairs.

"Okay, Mom, we'll be down in a couple of minutes," he replied, holding Drea's gaze.

She lowered her lids to hide her disappointment. She rolled over and pushed back the sheet to get out of bed.

"Drea?"

"I'll only be a couple of minutes in the bathroom, then it'll be all yours."

Avoiding his eyes, she snatched up some clothes and hurried across the hall. Closing the door behind her, she leaned against it for a long moment. Wow, what a way to wake up!

Drea dressed quickly and went downstairs to help Peggy with breakfast. She glanced at Keith when he joined them, but saw no hint of what he was thinking.

She refused to let him know how she felt. She still remembered his mocking laughter when she'd been a teenager. She couldn't bear that now.

When they reached the hospital, Keith gave Drea the keys to the car.

"You drive Mom home when she wants to go. I'm going to check on Dad, then head for the site. I'll borrow one of the company pickup trucks to use until we get a car of our own."

"Do you want me to drive you there?"

"No, I called Ben at work. He'll pick me up. Stay with Mom as long as she needs you, okay?"

Drea nodded.

"I don't need anyone to babysit me, Keith. Once Drea sees Matt, she can go on home and work on her book if she needs to. I'm planning to stay all day. I brought my knitting and a book to read. Just pick me up in time for dinner," his mother said.

"What time did Becky say to be there?"

"Around six-thirty."

"Okay, I'll go home and shower after work. Then Drea and I will swing by here to pick you up," Keith said. "Does that suit you, Drea?"

She nodded.

He smiled again and leaned closer. "Chatty again?"

She looked at those lips, remembering last night. Her eyes dancing, she glanced up to meet his. And nodded.

He chuckled and flung his arm around her shoulder. "Go check Dad, Mom. He'll be anxious to see you."

"You should go first since you have to leave for the site."

"No, I can wait. It's more important for him to see his wife first. Just don't stay all day."

She smiled and hurried down the hall.

"I can give you a ride to the site," Drea said as Keith led her into the waiting room. It was deserted.

"No need. Ben and I have things we can discuss on the ride over. I'll be home before six."

"Okay."

He paused near the window and glanced over his shoulder. Seeing no one around, he turned Drea around and kissed her gently.

"Didn't get a chance to do that earlier."

His husky voice splashed through her like heated wine. She smiled and shook her head. The unexpected kiss made up for some of her earlier disappointment.

He kissed her again and again—light, sipping kisses. A mere touching of lips to lips, to cheeks, to forehead. Back to lips, he deepened the kiss slightly. Always aware of where they were and that they might be interrupted at any moment, Keith made sure the embrace didn't get out of hand.

"Mmm," Drea murmured.

"Mmm?" Keith repeated, resting his forehead against hers and gazing down into her pretty brown eyes.

"Nice."

"More than nice. Let's head back home after we see Dad. We'll have the house to ourselves and can take up where Mom interrupted this morning."

"Mmm. But I've got to get to work."

She blinked at that, then giggled softly. One day she'd stop wishing he'd say what she wanted to hear and accept things the way they were.

"Yes you need to get to the work site. Get it straightened out for your dad."

She toyed with the button at the top of his shirt.

He took hold of her hand and gently pulled it away.

"If you want to change the rules, I'm game. Taking this any farther isn't what either of us signed up for with this marriage that not really a marriage."

Not really married. He'd proposed this marriage in exactly that way and saw it in those terms.

She sighed.

Was she fighting a useless battle?

And if she did change the rules, would that change the outcome? Would he forever see this as a temporary marriage to end before too long?

"There you two are. Matt's awake, though still groggy with all the painkillers. Go on in and see him, Keith. I'll go back after you and Drea have a chance to visit with him." Peggy bustled into the waiting room, her face bright and relaxed after satisfying herself that her husband was doing all right.

Keith turned without another word to head down the hall. He was floored at his reaction to Drea's kisses.

Did he want to change the rules of their agreement?

They'd married for convenience. *His* convenience. Now that the need was gone, they could get a quiet annulment and go their separate ways. He had no hold on Drea, nor did she owe him any loyalty beyond the terms they'd agreed to.

Even now she was thinking of finding another husband.

She didn't need to rush into anything. Maybe they'd stay married the full three years. He could see advantages to it. After all, they'd done well in Kuwait, sharing interests in common, enjoying the same activities.

He took a deep breath and pushed open the door to his father's room. Time enough later to think of the situation with his wife. He had a job to do to help out his father. One problem at a time.

Ten minutes later Keith left his father's room at the request of the nurse who wanted to run some tests. He leaned casually against the wall beside the door, waiting until he could go back inside.

It was disturbing to see his father laid low like that. All his life his dad had seemed like such a strong, invincible force. This heart attack and operation had shown Keith that his father was a man like any other, susceptible to the same illnesses and limitations.

And his father needed him now. Needed to be able to count on him, depend on his strength. It was payback time and Keith was ready and able and glad for the opportunity.

A movement down the hall caught his attention. Drea was walking toward the room. He watched her draw closer, a honey-sweet woman he wanted to clasp in his arms and never let go. Her walk was feminine and sexy, yet she hadn't a clue. Her wide-eyed innocence grabbed a man's heart and wouldn't turn it loose.

She'd hung on his every word last night, making him feel like a giant.

She'd poured herself into their kisses, until he thought he'd explode.

Pushing away from the wall, he walked to meet her.

Chapter Twelve

"Is Matt all right?" she asked, peering toward his father's room.

"The nurse is with him."

Keith reached out and took her arm, pulling her around to the wall, leaning over her, resting his forearm on the cool tile, sheltering her from anyone who happened to glance down the wide hallway.

"Did you want me to go back to the waiting room?" she asked breathlessly.

Every time she was close to him she had trouble with her breathing. She tightened her hands into fists to keep from reaching out to touch him, to link herself with him, however tenuously.

He shook his head.

"Your friend Ben is in the waiting room. That's what I came to tell you."

"I'm the boss. Maybe I'll take a day off."

"You just started."

He bent his head and met her waiting lips, covering them, searching for the hot-honey warmth of her with his lips. She arched against him, pushing away from the wall, straining to meet the flare of passion that rose at his touch.

The soft chiming of the hospital intercom brought them back to reality. Down the hall a nurse pushed a cart.

Drea broke the kiss by turning her head and pushing against his chest. He stepped back.

"Go with Ben," Drea said softly, her hand lingering on his chest as if reluctant to break contact.

Keith ran his fingers through his hair and stared down at her. He wanted her in the worst way, more than he'd wanted any woman before. She was pretty, sexy and exuded such an air of innocence.

Yet her responses to his kisses were anything but innocent. She had fiery depths he wanted to plumb. She had a look about her that heated his blood until he thought he'd burn up. And soon he was going to do just that, with her. Burn them both up.

"Until later, then."

She nodded with a smile, finally drawing her hand away.

"You can count on it," she said.

Drea watched him walk away, wanting to dance for joy in the hallway. He wanted her, that was clear. After all these years, he wanted her. For a night, a week, however long, she'd relish every single second with him. It was so much more than she'd ever thought she'd have.

Yet it was still less than what she wanted.

She wanted it all. One way or another, she was going to do her best to get happy ever after!

As Drea loosened the angel food cake from the pan that afternoon, she could feel the perspiration dripping. It was hot!

She wondered for the tenth time in ten minutes why Peggy and Matt had never put in central air-conditioning. Virginia was notorious for its hot and humid summers. The window units in the bedrooms made sleeping comfortable, but the kitchen needed one more than any other room. Especially when baking.

She dusted off the crumbs and studied the cake. She should have been writing. But she couldn't concentrate.

Instead of the computer screen, she saw Keith.

Instead of correcting the dialogue of her hero, she heard the words she wish Keith would say.

She was slowly going crazy. Crazy with longings and rising desire.

In hopes that baking would give her something else to think about, she'd decided to make a cake to take to Becky's tonight.

Now she was ready to frost the angel food cake with strawberries in whipped cream. The frosting was light, just a bit sweet and a perfect complement to the cake. They'd have to keep it in the cooler to take to Becky's. She hoped it wasn't too hot for the cream to whip.

She brushed her forehead with her arm. Drawing the chilled bowl and beaters from the refrigerator, she mashed the strawberries. Taking the heavy cream out, she began to whip it. The drone of the mixer filled the air as she slowly turned the bowl.

It was getting close to six o'clock. Keith would be home soon.

She still had to change her clothes before she was ready.

The old shorts and skimpy top she wore wouldn't do at all for dinner. But it was the coolest thing she had for work in the hot kitchen.

She'd pinned up her hair to keep it from getting in her way. It was damp with the heat. The soft scooped-neck top buttoned up the front and she'd left a few buttons undone top and bottom to permit maximum circulation of any air that might be stirring.

Did Peggy have a fan somewhere? If not, then Drea would invest in one.

She dipped her finger into the bowl, tasted the whipped cream. It was thick enough for the strawberries. She added some, mixed them in. Just about—

The hand on her shoulder scared her half to death. With a shriek, Drea whirled around, pulling the hand-held mixer from the bowl, splattering whipped cream and strawberries on everything within five feet.

"Keith! My gracious you scared me half to death!"

Quickly she snapped off the mixer, looked in dismay at the mess on the counter, the wall, Keith and herself.

He grinned. "I called to you when I walked in, but I guess you didn't hear me."

"I certainly didn't. Look at this mess. I don't have time for this!"

She slammed the mixer on the counter and reached for a damp dishcloth.

He reached out and stopped her, turning her around until she faced him.

"I'm sorry. I thought you heard me."

He studied her face for a long moment, his eyes locking with hers.

"You have whipped cream here."

He touched the corner of her mouth. Leaning over, he licked the cream off.

Drea's anger instantly changed entirely. She felt his tongue brush across her skin, tasting her, tasting the strawberries and cream. Her heart skidded in her chest.

"You have some here." He licked her cheek.

She was flushed from the heat in the kitchen, her scent mingled with that of the freshly baked cake and the sweet strawberries in the cream. He brought his hands up to hold her shoulders as he traced his tongue across her cheek, licking away every splash of whipped cream.

"Keith," she whispered, her eyes closed as she enjoyed the exquisite sensations jostling through her. He needed to stop before she was a quivering mass of nerves and cravings. But she couldn't tell him that.

"And here."

His tongue moved down her throat, his lips closing over her skin, his hot, open, wet kisses driving the heat in her body to a critical level.

"Keith." she tried again.

Her knees were weak, her body pliant and soft. She wanted to sink into a puddle on the floor and pull him with her. Lights whirled behind her closed lids. Delight spread as his mouth continued to touch her, caress her, drive her wild with increasing desire.

As if they had all the time in the world, he picked her up

and set her on the edge of the counter. Tilting her head back, he continued his assault on her throat, coming time and time again to the rapid pulse point.

"Stop."

Drea wished she had more force behind her voice. Intellectually she knew they had to stop, but every cell in her body cried out for more. Threading her fingers into his hair, she held him close to her, telling him to stop, yet belying the command by holding him so he could not.

"Just checking to make sure I get all that cream," he murmured.

She loved him, had loved him since she'd been a girl of sixteen. Now, after all these years, now he noticed her, drove her deep into passion as he led her to heights never before dreamed about.

"I told you about your hair," he whispered in her ear as he unfastened it from the topknot that held it off her neck.

The soft waves cascaded down, blanketing her, holding in the heat that his touch built.

"It was cooler that way," she whispered, her lips tracing his jaw.

His mouth found hers in another wild and wonderful kiss.

"Keith? Drea? Oh, my."

Peggy Branson stopped in stunned surprise at the back door.

Keith broke the kiss and stepped back.

"I'm so sorry. I didn't mean to interrupt," Peggy said.

"It's all right, Mom. I thought we were picking you up at

the hospital."

Keith glanced at Drea. Her face was crimson. He wanted to say something, but didn't know the words to ease her embarrassment.

"I got a ride home. I thought I'd change into something that didn't smell like the hospital to go to Becky's. I'm sorry I interrupted."

She walked quickly through the kitchen.

"Although—" she paused at the door to the dining room and looked at both of them with a huge grin "—there's nothing wrong in my book with a man showing his love to his wife."

With a small laugh, she turned and headed for her room.

Chapter Thirteen

"**D**rea?"

"Go take your shower. We don't have much time if we want to get to Becky by six-thirty," she said stiffly, hopping off the counter and picking up the mixer and switching it on.

Keith's hand covered hers. He flicked off the beaters.

"Are you all right?"

"Sure."

She kept her gaze on the whipped cream, internally screaming for him to leave before she fell apart.

He cupped her chin and brought her face around, his eyes penetrating. "Embarrassed?"

She nodded. "I can't believe your mom walked in on us like that."

"She didn't seem perturbed. If anything, it reaffirmed her belief in our marriage. Wasn't that the purpose of your kiss a couple days ago?"

"That was different."

"Not as intense, that's for sure," he teased gently.

She flushed. "Go get dressed and let me finish the cake. We're going to be late."

"So what? We won't be that late, and besides, Becky's family. We'll just tell her—"

"We won't tell her anything. "Go!"

She glared at him, but he was totally unaffected.

Grinning cheekily, he dropped a quick kiss on her lips and turned to saunter from the room as if he had all the time in the world.

Turning back to the cake, Drea wondered if she could slink off to bed and hide under the covers and never have to face her mother-in-law again.

Being in Keith's arms drove every bit of sense from her mind.

Peggy entered the kitchen just as Drea finished spreading the last of the frosting. She walked over to the younger woman.

"I'm sorry I interrupted, Drea," she began.

"We shouldn't have been doing that here," Drea said, avoiding the other woman's eyes.

"It did me good to see it, though. I sometimes worried about your marriage. Your wedding seemed like such a rushed affair, just when he got his new job and all. I realize you couldn't wait, but I was worried all the same."

"We did rush, but everything's fine," Drea said.

The last thing she wanted was for Keith's parents to suspect everything wasn't perfect in their world. They didn't need additional worry at this stage. Time enough for them to learn the truth if they went through with the annulment.

If?

When.

"Let me help you get that into the cooler," Peggy offered when Drea finished.

"Thanks."

If her mother-in-law was offering an olive branch, Drea was willing to take it. It'd still be a long time before Drea forgot her embarrassment, however.

"I still need to change. You might want to give Becky a call and tell her we're running a little late."

Drea hurried up the stairs and into the bedroom. She paused only a moment when she saw Keith buttoning his shirt. His slacks were still unzipped, awaiting his shirttails. She brushed past him to go to the closet and pull out a sundress.

"Let's send Mom to Becky's alone and finish what we started downstairs."

She stared down at the white dress with the little blue flowers scattered throughout. Flicking a glance at Keith, she wished again he'd just once say something she wanted to hear.

"Want me to leave you to dress in private?" he asked.

She nodded, laying the dress across the end of the bed. She'd take a quick sponge bath, to freshen up a little before dressing. Give herself time to cool down.

He nodded, his eyes serious. "Okay this time, honey, but not forever."

"What do you mean?"

"I mean I think we should move forward in this relationship. Not like it was in Kuwait."

He stopped by the door and looked back at her. "I want you, Drea."

That came close to what she wanted to hear. She nodded. There was no use denying the obvious truth. She smiled as hope rose.

"So what are we going to do?"

"Show you later."

Drea stared at the closed door for a long moment, her imagination flying in a hundred different directions. A glance at the clock had her hurrying to get dressed.

Dinner was a joyful affair. With everyone relieved that Matt's prognosis was so favorable, they were able to relax and enjoy the meal. Trevor and Tyler were the center of attention. They were exuberant, outgoing little boys, quick to make friends. After climbing into their grandmother's lap to share special treats with her, they made the rounds.

Keith picked up Trevor when he came over, smiling at his nephew. He was a sturdy boy, easily recognized as Tom's son. He proudly showed Keith his truck and explained how he liked to play with it in the sandbox. Maybe his uncle would go out after dinner and see how it worked, he slyly suggested.

Keith glanced up to see Tyler snuggled up in Drea's lap, regaling her with stories about a nest of baby birds the boys could see from their bedroom window. She leaned over him, totally absorbed in the toddler's tale.

Keith's heart jerked as he watched. For the first time in years he thought about a family of his own.

He knew Drea wanted one. She'd said that was the reason she'd look for another husband as soon as their marriage was over. She wanted children, wanted a family to love and belong to.

Until she found someone, she'd be all alone when they separated.

A family. A baby. He'd wanted kids, years ago. Diane always put off starting a family, saying the time wasn't right. He was glad now that she had. Divorce was hard on kids.

Drea would be a wonderful mother. He could see her cuddling their own child as she was holding Tyler.

Their own child?

No, he dared not create a baby with her. Not unless they decided to stay married. And that was still up in the air. He knew intellectually that Drea was nothing like Diane. She didn't gamble. He knew she wasn't seeing anyone on the side.

Yet a part of him was afraid to really let go and trust. She'd gone into this marriage with certain expectations. They'd married for business reasons.

Would she want to stay married to him? Would she want to start a family with him?

He was almost thirty-two years old. His father'd had two kids by the time he was thirty-two. Becky was the same age as Drea and would have three children in another couple of months. No wonder Drea didn't want to waste any time finding a mate. Neither one of them was getting younger.

Slowly he turned his attention back to Trevor, but in the back of his mind remained the idea of staying married, starting a family, seeing what life had to offer with Drea by his side.

After dinner, Becky sent the boys out in the backyard to play while the adults had dessert and coffee.

"I love angel food cake and the whipped-cream frosting is great," she said as she handed around the plates.

"I'm fond of it, too—wherever I find it," Keith murmured, sitting beside Drea.

She smiled up at Becky, ignoring Keith, though she tingled in response to the memory his low voice triggered. She finally threw him a glance from beneath her lashes, pleased to find he was studying her.

"And this is for both of you from all of us."

Becky handed Drea a large envelope, with a bright silver bow on top.

"What is it?" Drea asked, looking at her friend.

Becky grinned and settled awkwardly down beside Tom.

"It's a wedding present. You and Keith married so fast last summer we didn't have time to think up something great. But we have now and want you to have it."

"We didn't need wedding gifts," Keith said slowly, eyeing the envelope.

"Maybe you didn't, brother dear. It wasn't your first wedding, but it was Drea's and she deserves something."

Becky's glare dared him to argue.

Keith nodded and watched as Drea slowly opened the envelope flap.

"Oh!"

She stared at the gift certificate then looked up at Keith, her expression uncertain.

"What is it?"

"A long weekend at the Sun and Sea Hotel at Virginia Beach," she said, naming one of the more exclusive hotels in that resort town.

"Nice."

His gaze held hers. He could envision her stretched out on the sand, wearing some skimpy bikini. He'd rub oil on her back, down to her hips, along the backs of her legs. Keith cleared his throat and looked away, before his thoughts betrayed him in front of everyone.

"Thanks, Becky," Drea said, "Thanks to both of you. This is wonderful."

"Well, no matter what you say, I don't think Kuwait is the ideal honeymoon spot. Now you can take a long weekend, once Dad's better and Keith can break away from work," Becky said brightly. "Or when you hit the New York Times best-seller list again."

"New York Times best-seller list?" Keith asked.

Drea's heart sank. She'd never gotten around to telling him. She wished he didn't have to learn about it this way.

Becky stared at her. "Didn't you tell him?"

"Not yet," Drea said.

It had been stupid, not telling him. She'd wanted him to ask, but he never had.

"Not yet?" Tom sat up and asked. "The first one was a year ago."

He turned to Keith. "Your wife's quite famous. Both her first two books hit the best-seller list within weeks of publication."

"I didn't know," Keith said quietly, his eyes on Drea. "She didn't mention it."

Something cold settled around his heart. Here he'd been thinking about staying married to Drea and she'd never even mentioned such a momentous event like her books reaching the New York Times list.

Obviously she wasn't planning to continue in the

marriage.

Did she want to end it now that they were back in the States? She'd mentioned it, but he'd wanted to keep looking after her.

Now he wasn't sure what he wanted, what she wanted.

Drea looked around. Everyone was staring at her, waiting to hear her explanation of why she hadn't related such an important event to her husband. Peggy looked worried and confused. Becky's look was challenging, Tom's puzzled. Keith's eyes were narrowed as he gazed impassively at her.

Drea took a deep breath and turned to Keith.

"Actually it was hard to realize over in Kuwait. I mean I got a note from my agent. And you were so busy with work and everything. I, uh, I guess it just never seemed the right time to bring it up. You never asked how things were going, so I guess I thought you wouldn't be interested. I'm sorry if I was wrong."

Keith nodded and looked away.

Now he was the one embarrassed. Not once in an entire year had he asked about her writing. He'd dictated the terms of their marriage, he'd set the pace for their life in Kuwait. No wonder she'd never brought it up—she'd ample reason to suspect he wouldn't be interested.

But it made him almost sick to realize something so exciting had happened to her and she'd believed him so disinterested in her life that she wasn't comfortable enough to share it with him.

He was a fool. He'd thought maybe they could continue being married.

He'd never thought that Drea might not wish to continue.

"How is your current book coming?" Peggy asked, trying to fill the awkward silence.

"I'm doing the last of the revisions."

"Do you have an idea for the next one?" Tom asked.

"I'm playing with some ideas in my head. Once I finish the revisions, I'll try to draw up a proposal for the next one."

"Still using John Taylor as the hero?"

Drea nodded, glancing at Keith.

His expression was closed. He stared down at his coffee. Her heart went out to him. She wouldn't have embarrassed him before his family for anything. She should have told him before, whether or not he wanted to hear it.

Now it was too late.

When the boys trooped back inside, the atmosphere lightened. Drea's books were not mentioned again.

When they were leaving, Keith drew his sister aside. "I assume you have copies of Drea's books. Can I borrow one to read?"

Becky started to say something, but only nodded and went to fetch the books. Handing them to Keith, she looked sympathetic.

"Thanks, Sis. I'll return them when I finish reading them."

"You could have asked Drea. I know she'd have been delighted to have you read her books."

"I should have," was all he said.

Keith bade his mother and Drea good-night when they reached home, then headed for his father's home office, closing the door firmly behind him.

"I guess I blew that, huh?" Drea said as she heard the door

click shut.

"I'm not sure. He could have asked. Isn't that what you were waiting for?" Peggy said.

Drea nodded her head.

"Sometimes men can be very self-centered. It doesn't mean that they don't love us or care about what we do. They just forget, I guess," Peggy said.

"It's all right, Peggy. Keith had lots to do in Kuwait. And I should have told him. It was stupid to wait for him to ask. Obviously he thought it wasn't important to me because I never talked about my books. I hope he doesn't feel hurt that I didn't tell him."

"You and he need to work this out for yourselves. You don't need nosy in-laws interfering. Good night, my dear. Will you be taking me to the hospital in the morning?"

"Yes. We'll plan to be there by nine. I'll visit Matt for a few minutes, then I have to get back to work."

Drea took a shower before putting on her T-shirt. Once in the large bed, she reached for her notepad. She added sexy nightgown to her growing list. It was time she stopped sleeping in Keith's shirt and found something more alluring. When they left his parents' home, chances were good they'd revert to separate bedrooms again. She didn't have much time.

Lying down, she listened to the sounds of the old house settling for the night. Her tenants would be moving out soon and she could move back home.

She missed her house. She'd be glad to go back home.

Would Keith still go with her? Did he want to stay married? Tonight demonstrated how far apart they truly were. Could they bridge the gap and draw closer?

She shook her head to clear it. They needed to talk.

And Keith was not a man for talking.

Sighing softly, Drea began to think about a new plot line for her next book. She'd finish her line edit by the end of the week. She'd like to come up with at least an idea to pitch to her editor by then. Maybe the new story could involve construction.

Immediately she saw Keith as he had been the other afternoon—hard hat, tool belt and masculine stance. Should John Taylor work undercover as a construction worker for this book? She'd never had a permanent love angle. John found a woman in each book to help him and to offer a fleeting love interest. Was it time to change that?

She sat up and reached for her notebook, jotting down plot points. When finished, she tossed the notebook on the bedside table and switched off the light. She wasn't waiting up for Keith tonight.

Instead she dreamed about the next story idea, mixing construction with underworld crime, dusty pickups with fancy foreign cars. The blossom of her idea was beginning to unfold.

Chapter Fourteen

Keith leaned his head back against the recliner and closed his eyes. He wanted to finish the book tonight but didn't think he'd make it. The words danced before his eyes. Maybe if he rested a bit, he could continue.

It was after one. He needed to get some sleep if he planned to be alert on the job in the morning.

Who'd have suspected his shy, innocent, sweet wife capable of writing such a powerful book?

Drea had never gone anywhere except college in Charlottesville, never done anything except work as a librarian and take care of her father. Yet her writing was strong, clear and captivating. The research he understood. With her background, she'd know instantly how to locate any fact she needed.

What was so astonishing was the manner in which she was able to draw the reader into the dark underworld of crime and intrigue. The language was gritty and sparse, painting vivid scenes with few words, yet expressing every nuance needed to captivate the reader's attention.

He felt as if he were a part of John Taylor's experiences, as if he were right there with the hero.

And the twists and turns of the plot were masterful.

How had she known to do all that? And how was she going to let her hero find his way out of the convoluted situation he was in?

This book exposed an entirely new dimension to Drea.

Keith wanted to talk to her about her writing, find out how she did it. What had first encouraged her to even try to write? And where did she get her ideas?

After he finished this book he'd ask her.

He picked it up again and plunged back into the action.

When Drea awoke the next morning, the bed beside her was empty. She reached out—the sheets were cool. If Keith had come to bed, he'd left hours ago. Sighing softly, she rose and went to get dressed.

When she joined Peggy in the kitchen for breakfast, she asked after Keith.

"He left early. He said there was a lot to do at the site and he wanted to get some time in before going to see his dad. Apparently Matt's questioning him on what's going on and Keith wanted to have all the information available."

"He and Matt aren't arguing, are they?" Drea asked.

"I don't think so. I think Matt just wants to know things are getting back on track. We've talked a bit. I think he's going to give the business up. This heart attack changes the way we think about things. Life's too precious to live with problems we don't need. If Keith wants to take over, I think Matt's ready to let him."

"Keith will make changes," Drea warned.

"Matt knows that. He's ready to let go. He wouldn't place

any restrictions if he turns the company over to him. Do you think Keith would take it?"

Drea nodded. "If he could have total freedom to run it as he wants, I think he would. He might be a bit stubborn about structuring the deal so he doesn't feel Matt is just giving it to him."

"But why not? Why else does he think Matt built it up except to leave it to Keith?"

"They'll have to work that out between themselves. I know Keith has a strong streak of independence. He doesn't like depending on anyone or feeling as if he's been given a handout."

"Then let's hope Matt knows that, as well."

When they arrived at the hospital, Matt was much improved. Many of the tubes had been removed. Only the IV and one cardiac monitor remained. He was sitting up in bed and his color was almost back to normal.

Drea was glad for the improvement. It meant more to see him this way than to hear the doctor say he'd recover. She visited for a few minutes, then gave him a quick kiss on the cheek, saying she'd see him later. She knew he and Peggy wanted to be together.

Revisions went a little easier. But instead of fantasizing about Keith and his kisses, Drea found herself worrying from time to time about his reaction to the fact she hadn't told him about her books.

He hadn't said a word last night and that concerned her. Was he furious or hurt? Had he started to read one of her books last night? She'd seen the ones Becky gave him. He could have asked her—she had her author's copies just collecting dust in their boxes.

Had he come to bed at all last night or was he already pulling away?

She couldn't stand the uncertainty. Calling his cell, Drea waited impatiently for him to answer.

"Branson Construction," Keith said after two rings.

"Have you had lunch yet?" she asked.

"Drea? No, I haven't eaten."

"I could bring you something. We could have lunch together."

The silence stretched endlessly before he replied.

"I'd like that. Come around one. I'll take a break then."

She hung up almost giddy with relief. She went to the kitchen to see what kind of sumptuous lunch she could make.

When she arrived, he was working on the joists of one of the houses. Leaving the basket of food in the cool office, she went searching for him. Spotting him on the high beam, Drea was content to watch him work. He'd discarded his shirt and his skin gleamed in the hot sun. His tan was even and dark. She remembered glimpsing the lighter skin below his waist when he'd opened the bathroom door the other evening. She swallowed hard with the memory.

He saw her and waved. Finishing the job he was doing, he called something to the others working on the framing and climbed down the ladder.

"Lunch?" he asked, drawing near.

She nodded, letting her eyes boldly roam over his chest, down the long legs encased in snug jeans. Raising her gaze to meet with his, she let her appreciation show.

He smiled and reached out to capture the nape of her neck in his hand, drawing her close for a kiss.

He smelled of fresh cut wood and sunshine and male sweat. Drea drew in a deep breath, reveling in the heady sensations his touch always brought.

"So what's for lunch?" he said a moment later turning toward the trailer.

He shrugged into a shirt, then his hand drifted down to clasp with hers as they walked carefully across the construction site.

"Fried chicken, hot biscuits, iced tea and an orange."

"No cake?"

"We left it with Becky."

"Umm, wouldn't mind some of that whipped cream, never mind the cake."

He held the door open for her, his expression teasing.

Drea relaxed. It was going to be all right. He wasn't mad. He didn't seem hurt. He was the teasing man she so often found confusing to deal with.

When they made a makeshift table from the second desk and began to eat, Keith said, "I read one of your books last night, *Open the Gate to Death*."

"And?"

"I see why it hit the best-seller list. You've got a tremendous talent, honey."

"So you liked it?"

"I sure did. I have to read the second one tonight."

"You don't have to do that, you know."

She didn't want him to feel obligated to read her books.

"I want to. Then I'm going to cross-examine you like John Taylor does. How did you ever get into writing stories like this?"

She smiled and shrugged. "They just come to me. Although, I have to do tons of research. Especially for the first one—I didn't have a clue about guns and other weapons. But it filled the nights."

She snapped her mouth shut before she gave away the true reason she'd started writing. She'd never expected to marry while taking care of her father. She rarely dated and found the outlet of writing enough to give her a measure of contentment she hadn't expected.

"I've got another suggestion," he said.

She blinked. "What?"

Reaching out, he cupped her chin, tracing his thumb across her lower lip, tugging a little, brushing back and forth.

"Tonight, you and I are going to excuse ourselves early and go to bed. And we are *not* going to sleep."

"We're not?"

Her heart pounded in her chest, the blood surged through her veins.

Slowly he shook his head, his eyes looking deep into hers, desire clearly showing.

She gripped his wrist, holding on for dear life, lest she float away.

"What time are you coming home?" she asked softly.

"I'll be home by six. We'll eat, call to see how Dad's doing and go to our room for privacy."

Drea licked suddenly dry lips, touching her tongue against his thumb, tasting him, anticipation building sweet and strong. She wanted the afternoon to pass swiftly and night to fall fast. She wanted to savor the promise in his eyes, relish the growing excitement that swelled deep inside her. She felt the rising tension as the image of his words burned into her mind. She wanted the day to end—now.

"So are you writing this afternoon?" he asked settling back to eat.

"If I can concentrate," she said with a shy smile. "You didn't make that easy with your comment."

"I've been thinking about you since I woke up yesterday morning. Time enough now to end this suspense."

"I don't have much practice," she said with hesitation.

"We can practice together."

Drea took a deep breath. "Okay then."

She didn't know if thing would go as she imagined, but the fact he seemed interested lifted her spirits and hopes higher than ever.

Once lunch was over the afternoon would seem endless, but the sooner she got out of his way, the sooner he'd finish for the day and come home.

Besides, she wanted to do some shopping. Time to check some of the items off her list.

And moving up to the top of the list was a new nightgown. Something very feminine, very different from a utilitarian T-shirt.

By the time Drea finished shopping and returned home it was time to start dinner. There was a message on the answering machine from Peggy saying she wouldn't be home until late. Friends had joined her at the hospital and wanted to take her to dinner when she left for the day.

Drea played the message through a second time, her heart pounding with the implications. She and Keith wouldn't have to wait until bedtime if they didn't want to. Peggy wouldn't be home. The house would be theirs all evening.

Trying to ignore the pull of excitement that swept through her, Drea continued up the stairs to unpack her new clothes. She drew out the sexy nightie. It was pale peach, short, with lots of lace and ribbons. She felt like a new bride. Which she was, if truth be known. This would be her wedding night.

Spreading it out on the bed, she then pulled out the new shorts and top she hadn't been able to resist. She swiftly changed. The shorts were short, exposing the entire length of her legs. The top was cropped, ending above her waistband, exposing an inch or so of abdomen. It buttoned in the front. Would Keith wish to unfasten these buttons slowly, one at a time?

Brushing out her hair, she deliberately fastened it on top of her head again, letting wispy tendrils float down around her face. She glanced in the mirror, satisfied with the effect.

If he wanted to change the rules of the marriage, she was more than willing to accommodate him.

Chapter Fifteen

Drea decided to make a salad for dinner. That'd be quick and easy and not involve cooking. Since only the two of them would be home for dinner, they could eat in the backyard. She hoped that would prove more comfortable than eating in the warm kitchen.

She prepared a large garden salad, then sliced cold ham and turkey and cheese and mixed it all up. Whipping up a batch of corn bread, she plopped it into the oven just as Keith arrived home.

"Dinner'll be ready soon," she said as he walked into the kitchen, feeling a sudden attack of shyness hit her.

His eyes gleamed at the sight of her shorts, the cropped top. Smiling, he strode quickly across the room. Tipping up her chin, he brushed his lips across hers.

"Why wait for dinner? You look good enough to eat right now."

She pushed gently against his shoulder, warmth from his words matching the heat from the oven.

"Go take your shower, but make it quick. The corn bread will be ready in about fifteen minutes."

He was back in ten.

"Your mother's eating out with friends tonight," Drea told him when he rejoined her. "Would you like beer or iced tea to drink?"

"Tea. When is she coming home?"

Keith leaned against the counter, watching Drea move around the kitchen. Wearing cutoff jeans and a short-sleeved, cotton shirt left unbuttoned, he was as cool as he was going to get this evening. And watching his sexy little wife was raising his temperature.

His eyes were drawn to the smooth expanse of legs revealed by her shorts. The way the cotton clung to the gentle swell of her hips made his hand yearn to touch her. He wasn't sure he wanted dinner.

He was sure he wanted Drea.

"Late. I hope she can enjoy herself."

"Huh?"

He'd missed part of what she'd said, thinking of getting her in bed, of peeling off that skimpy little top, slipping her out of those indecently short shorts and kissing every inch of her delectable body.

Drea eyed him suspiciously. "I said your mother would be late getting home."

"Good."

He pushed away from the counter and walked over to her, reaching out to draw her into his arms.

The afternoon was sultry but the heat from Keith was scorching. Drea opened her mouth under his and pressed eagerly against him, feeling the hard, sleek muscles of his chest. Only the soft cotton of her top separated them. The potency of his kisses curled her toes.

Beneath his talented mouth, the kitchen faded from her consciousness. His kisses carried her to a magical place of unexpected pleasure. He inflamed her, captivated her, as she spiraled to heightened awareness. He brought forth the secret yearnings and cravings that had been buried deep within her. His special touch awoke her to enchantments never before known.

The steady ding-ding of the oven timer finally penetrated, pushed back the sensual haze. Slowly she pulled back.

"Keith, I have to get the corn bread. It'll burn otherwise."

"Umm. Let it."

His mouth captured hers again.

She kissed him briefly, the pulled back.

"Stop. Let me get the corn bread out."

Pulling away, Drea spun around to silence the annoying timer. Pulling open the oven door, she was enveloped by the heat. It still didn't compare to her own temperature when Keith was kissing her.

Lifting out the pan, she set it on the counter.

"Don't you want dinner?" she asked. "I made a big salad and thought we could eat outside."

Keith looked once more at her mouth, as if he'd forget dinner and take her in his arms again. But he shrugged. "Sure, sounds good."

Working together, they soon had the meal on the old picnic table beneath the large oak behind the house. Conversation was easy between them as they enjoyed the pleasant coolness in the yard. The old oak trees offered shelter from the heat of the waning afternoon sun. The high hedges on both sides offered total privacy from the neighbors. Farther back, the yard sloped down to a small wooded area. As the sun sank in the west, twilight cloaked them in a warm intimate world of two.

The evening reminded Drea of some of the better memories she had of Kuwait. The ones where Keith had come home for dinner and stayed to talk to her rather than returning to work or going to bed early. Such evenings had been rare and she had cherished them all the more when they'd come.

They discussed his dad's prognosis and how soon he might be released from the hospital. Keith spoke of the work going on at the Windmere site and related some of the problems facing Branson Construction.

Drea mentioned talking to the real estate agent about how soon her tenants might be expected to move out.

When they finished eating, they moved to the wooden swing. Drea wondered if Keith was as reluctant to end the pleasant evening as she was.

"Tired?" she asked sympathetically.

"Yeah."

He tilted his head back and closed his eyes. Strain and tension were evident in the lines beside his mouth, in the way he held himself.

Drea's heart ached as she sat beside him and sipped her iced tea. He gently pushed them back and forth in the swing. The silence was comfortable. The night was still and hot; the sun's setting had not cooled things off appreciably.

She gazed out over the colorful garden, enjoying the

serenity and peace. It reminded her of her own yard. She wondered how her flowers had fared with her tenants. She hoped they'd survived. She loved the various beds she'd planted in past years.

Drea sat quietly in the swing, growing more and more conscious of Keith sitting only inches away. She couldn't think of anything else to say. She could see his large capable hands holding his glass, raising it to his lips from time to time to sip. The same lips that had her mindless with sensations whenever they touched her. His legs were stretched out, moving just a little as he pushed the swing to and fro. His shirt had fallen open, his chest showing a deep tan against the soft blue of the shirt.

Tightening her hold on the cold glass, she resisted the urge to take up where they'd stopped in the kitchen. Was he waiting for some sign from her that she was ready to continue where they'd left off?

Keith looked over at her from beneath half-closed lids. He reached out and took her glass from her fingers and set both their glasses on the grass beneath the swing. Drea brushed her hands against her shorts to still their nervous energy.

"Come here," he said.

She hesitated only a moment. Then, taking a deep breath, she slowly moved, surprising Keith by daring to slip across his legs, sitting on his lap. Tilting her head, she studied him in the waning light, hoping he couldn't feel her rapid heartbeat.

It was twilight, the soft time of day when things blurred as the light faded from the sky. Soon it'd be dark. But for now there was plenty of soft seductive light to see by.

"Well?" he asked, a lopsided smile on his face as his eyes gazed into hers. His hands rested on her legs.

"Well."

She took a deep breath, wondering if she could go through with it. All day she'd been on tenterhooks of anticipation. He'd indicated they'd make love tonight. She wanted it as much as he did, maybe more.

Slowly, her eyes never leaving his, her right hand came up to the top button of her shirt. She slid it through the hole.

Keith guessed her intent. His smile faded as he watched her. His gaze flicked to the top of her shirt, back to her eyes.

The hunger Drea saw reflected there excited her. Slowly, Drea's hand slid down to the next button and slid it through its hole. The shirt opened slightly in a small V at the top.

She undid two more buttons, never taking her eyes from his. Her fingers trembled slightly. She hoped she wasn't making a fool of herself. But she wanted this too much to stop. Now the dark shadow of her cleavage began to show as the cropped top opened in a wider V, peeling down as it was released from the fasteners.

Keith watched Drea unfasten yet another button. His eyes gleamed in the twilight. Slowly her hand moved to the next one.

Her heart filled with love. She so wanted to make love with him, at least one time. To show him what she could not say. To love him.

Another button.

"Drea."

"Your top's open, shouldn't mine be?" she said softly, as yet another button slid from its hole.

"You're driving me crazy, honey," Keith said hoarsely.

She smiled at his tone and her hand slid to the next button. Her left hand reached out to push his shirt a bit off his shoulder, trace her fingertips down his chest. His hands tightened. Drea undid another button. Only two more remained.

The soft twilight was gone and only the hot dark night surrounded them, enclosed them. Heat enveloped them. She was intoxicated with the sensations Keith's touch induced, soaring beyond the realms of reality to the rapture that beckoned.

It had grown dark, quiet, still. She barely discerned him silhouetted against the slight light spilling out from the kitchen. Her heart pounded and she drew in ragged gulps of air to cool her heated body. They were concealed in darkness—the soft warm darkness of a Southern night, the soft warm delight of love.

Slowly, she began to come back to earth to grow cognizant of her surroundings. The grass beneath her was crushed, its fragrance permeating the heat surrounding them.

She began to relax, tracing lazy circles on his muscular back, relishing the feel of his sweat-soaked muscles beneath her fingertips.

He brushed his mouth against hers.

Drea kissed his neck, moved one hand up to play with his hair. She. "That was nice," she said softly.

"Oh, no." Keith closed his eyes. How could he have been

so carried away?

"What?"

"I didn't use anything for birth control," he said, rising up on his elbow to try to see her again.

She turned on her side, away from him, her knees drawn up against her chest. "It's okay," she said softly.

"You're on something?" he asked for clarification.

She shook her head. "No, but it'll be okay."

"Wrong time of the month?"

She rolled onto her back, turning her head to gaze at him. Keith reached out and took her hand in his as if needing some connection between them.

"It's too late to worry about anything, but I think I'm safe."

For one glorious moment she wondered what it'd be like to be pregnant with Keith's baby. She'd love to be the mother of his child, of his children. He'd make such a wonderful father.

"It would complicate our arrangement if you became pregnant," he said.

For a moment she felt a wave of sadness. He didn't want to be trapped into marriage. Would he feel that way if she were pregnant?

Later, when she was alone, she'd think it all through.

"Want to go upstairs?" he asked, rubbing her hand with his thumb.

"Yes."

She sat up and felt around for her clothes.

"We probably should get inside before your mother returns home. I don't want to traipse through her house with grass in my hair and stained and wrinkled clothes. How would we explain that?"

He chuckled, standing, then reached down to haul her to her feet. "If we're real lucky, we can make a dash for it now and not bother to get dressed."

She giggled softly, the adventure of the evening spiking through her veins. She picked up everything. "I'm game if you are. I get the shower first."

Drea turned and ran swiftly toward the gleaming light of the kitchen.

When Drea gained the safety of the bathroom, she sighed.

It had been wonderful! Would he make love to her again when they were in bed?

She ran the shower and stepped beneath the warm water. Before she could reach for the soap, however, Keith pushed back the curtain and stepped inside.

"Keith, what are you doing?"

"Saving Mom some water. Want me to wash your back?"

Drea bit her lip, then nodded and handed him the soap. This was more than she'd ever expected. She'd hold on to tonight's memories with both hands.

When the water began to run cold, he turned it off. Drying off, he opened the door and listened for any sounds of his mother's return. Apparently she was still visiting with her friends or had gone back to the hospital.

He turned and picked Drea up, cradling her against his chest.

"Keith!"

"Yes?"

"I can walk."

"Indulge me." He closed their bedroom door behind them and laid her on the bed.

Even before his breathing was steady again he knew she'd fallen asleep. Lying sprawled beside him like a boneless rag doll, her breathing was deep and even.

Keith kissed her gently on her mouth and rolled to his side, gathering her up to sleep in his arms.

Chapter Sixteen

Drea awoke the next morning knowing something was different. For a long moment she lay cocooned in the warmth of Keith arms, wondering what it was. Then she remembered last night.

Opening her eyes, she turned her head until she could see him. He was still sleeping, one arm across her as if holding her. The sheet was kicked away and they lay only in the warmth of the early-morning sun. Last night had been the most wonderful experience of her life. She smiled slightly in remembrance. He'd been a fantastic lover.

Only there had been no words of love.

None from him.

None from her.

She was afraid to say anything unless he spoke first.

The painful memories of her teenage years surfaced. She couldn't forget how he'd laughed with those other boys when discussing the crush she'd had.

Only it had been love even back then.

Had anything changed because of last night? For her it had been a joining of her soul to his. Was it only a joining of two bodies to him?

Had last night changed anything for him or was he still planning to end their temporary marriage once his father was fully recovered?

She slipped from the bed, careful not to awaken him. The future was too nebulous to consider right now. She'd draw on the patience that she'd learned when her father had been so ill, and wait and see.

"Good morning, Peggy. How was your dinner out?" Drea greeted her mother-in-law when she walked into the kitchen a short time later, dressed for the hospital.

"Hi, honey. It was quite nice. Marjorie and Pam stopped by the hospital first and spent a few minutes with Matt. Then we went to that new fish place down on Granby. Goodness, we got to talking and catching up on all the news until it was after eleven when we left. I've been so tied up with Matt I've let my friends slide."

"I'm sure they understand. It looks as if it did you good to go out ."

Drea smiled, noting the animation in Peggy's face.

"I'm starting to feel more normal. Each day that passes lets me believe just a little more that the doctor knows what he's talking about when he says Matt will be fine."

"Oh, Peggy, I'm sure the doctor wouldn't have said it if he didn't mean it."

Once again Drea imagined how she'd feel if it had been Keith so dangerously near death. She'd have been afraid, too.

"I know, but it was so hard, almost losing Matt like that. I think I'll live with that fear for a long time."

"Live with what a long time?"

Keith stepped into the kitchen. He gave his mother a quick kiss on her cheek, then turned to Drea. Drawing her into his arms as if he'd done it all his life, he kissed her, too.

"Good morning." His voice was low and husky, sending tantalizing waves of hunger along her nerves.

"Hi."

"I was saying I'll have to live with the fear of your father dying for a long time," his mother said, pouring him a cup of coffee. "Here, take this to the table. I'll have breakfast ready in a jiffy."

"You don't have to cook breakfast. I can do that," Drea protested.

"I'd like to. Then I want to go to the hospital." Peggy glanced over from the stove. "You two sure went to bed early last night. The house was dark when I got home."

Keith shrugged. "Still adjusting to this time zone, I guess." He winked at Drea.

She dropped her gaze to her coffee, wishing that they'd been alone. She should have waited for him to wake up. Maybe then she could have gotten some answers to the questions dancing around in her head. But she wouldn't voice them now. For the time being, she'd be patient.

When Drea and Peggy arrived at the hospital, they found Matt sitting up in bed, excited to be moving to the regular medical wing that morning.

"No more intensive cardiac care needed," he said proudly. "The doctor says I'm recovering in record time. Maybe I can even be discharged later this week."

"Oh, that would be so wonderful!" Peggy exclaimed.

Drea added her agreement, but wondered what it'd do to her relationship with Keith. Was Matt recovered enough to learn his son and his wife were separating? Or would he still need to be sheltered from such news for a while longer?

"Is Keith coming to see me tonight?" he asked.

"Yes. After work," Drea replied.

"It's so good to see you both. I'm glad you're back home where you belong. I didn't know I'd have to go to such lengths to get the two of you back, though."

She grinned at his joking. "We're glad to be back. I'm sorry you went to such lengths, too."

Matt reached for his wife's hand, held it in his as he looked shrewdly at Drea.

"I'm going to turn over Branson Construction to Keith. I'm retiring. This scare showed me how much I cherish life. From now on I'm going to do my best to enjoy whatever time I have left. I built up that business for him. Now I'm giving it to him."

Drea nodded, not knowing what to say.

"What will you do?" she asked.

Smiling up at Peggy, he answered, "Take a cruise for a start. Something we've talked about for years. Never managed it. We never had many vacations. I was too caught up in the company."

He leveled a glare at Drea. "Don't let Keith make the same mistakes. He needs to take vacations and delegate work. I should have learned that long ago."

"At least it's not too late now," Peggy said.

"We've been lucky," he said.

Feeling decidedly like a fifth wheel, Drea said goodbye and headed back for the house. She had lots to do. She'd been mooning around Keith Branson long enough. Time to get to work.

Keith stopped after work to visit his father.

"I didn't know they'd moved you," he said when he entered his father's semi private room that evening. The second bed was empty. Drawing up a chair, Keith sat close to his father's bed. No need to tell his dad that when he'd gone to the other room and found the bed empty he'd thought the worst for a second. He'd need his dad around for a long time.

"Glad you came by, son. I've got something to tell you. I'm signing over Branson Construction. As of today, it's all yours."

Keith sat up at that, staring at his father.

"You can't do that, Dad. It's your company. You've built it up from nothing to a very successful venture."

"Which has been faltering lately. I haven't had the energy to keep it up."

"That was because of your illness. Now that you're on the mend, you'll bounce back full of energy."

Matt shook his head.

"Maybe. But I don't want to focus all that energy on the company. I built up the company for you and Becky. It was always for you two. I'm signing it over to you now while you're young enough to make a difference with it. Some of the shares will go to your sister and I'll still want some income from it. But it'll be yours, lock, stock and barrel. You can put up your custom houses if that's what you want or continue in the housing development business as I did."

Keith was stunned. "I don't know, Dad—"

"Nothing to know. It's done, as soon as the attorney gets the papers for me to sign. It'll be yours—you can do whatever you want. Sell it if you don't want it."

Matt leaned back, studying his son.

"I'd never sell it! I don't know what to say," Keith said.

"Just say you'll make it the best dang construction company in the Tidewater."

"You mean, keep it the best in the Tidewater."

"Thanks, son. Did you hear that if I continue to improve as rapidly as I've done so far I'll be coming home at the end of the week?"

"That's great, Dad."

They talked for a little longer before Keith headed for home. He paused at the top of the hospital steps, his thoughts miles away.

With Drea, to be precise.

Slowly walking toward the company pickup truck, he wondered what his father's coming home would mean. It wouldn't be long before his dad and mom would no longer need to be sheltered from anything.

And before then, Keith needed to make up his mind what he wanted.

Dared he risk staying married?

I find I like being part of a couple. Drea words echoed in his mind. He liked being part of a couple, too, with Drea as the other part.

There was nothing saying he needed to make a decision today. They had plenty of time. It'd be weeks before his father was totally recovered. Time enough then to decide.

Drea was still at her computer when he arrived home. Swinging by the dining room, he watched her for a long moment before she knew he was there.

"Oh, hi. I didn't hear you."

She caught a glimpse of him from the corner of her eye and turned to smile at him.

Keith's gaze fastened on her mouth. Crossing the room in three long steps, he leaned over to kiss her.

"Writing going okay?" he asked a moment later.

"Yes. Today was very productive. How did things go at the site?"

"They're improving. Where's Mom?"

"She's at Becky's. She'll be home for dinner. I have a ham in the oven. You're home later than I expected."

"I went by to see Dad. I need to shower. Come up with me."

He reached for her hand, lacing his fingers with hers.

"All right." She pressed the save button and rose.

He wanted to tell her about his dad's decision, but something held him back. Was it a lack of trust?

He remembered Diane and how he'd once thought he could trust her but she'd betrayed him in every way. He dare not risk that devastation again.

Maybe he could trust Drea, but he hesitated. And that made him mad.

"I'll only be a few minutes," he said when he grabbed some clean clothes from the bedroom and headed for the shower.

Drea watched him leave, feeling a bit left out. Last night they'd showered together.

But not today.

Was he pulling back? Was he afraid after last night that she'd make demands? He'd made it clear a year ago he only wanted a temporary alliance. As he'd said last night, a baby would complicate things. Some of the warmth and glow of her day dimmed.

Nothing had changed with their agreement. Maybe he'd stay for the three years or maybe he'd be gone by the time his father returned home.

Whatever the outcome, she knew she'd love him until the day she died.

The next three weeks were busy. Drea finished her line edits and began her draft on a new book. Her notebook accompanied her everywhere as she jotted ideas down. Some were personal, such as how she could entice Keith into trusting her enough to give himself permission to fall in love with her. Others were notations she made to follow up on finding out more facts to use in the book.

She thought her husband cared for her. He'd made love to her almost every night. But was it enough? The patience she had counted on to carry her through was waning.

She longed to know exactly what his plans were, yet she was afraid to ask.

Matt came home from the hospital the end of that first week. He had exercises to do, special foods to eat and biweekly checkups to pass. But he was steadily improving.

While he tired easily and took a long nap every day, it was

obvious to everyone he was on the road to full recovery.

Keith worked hard at Branson Construction, sometimes slipping back into the routine he'd followed in Kuwait of working as long as there was daylight.

Her tenants found a new place and planned to move any day now, so her house would be available. On the day she found out, she drove to the Windmere site to tell Keith.

The construction had progressed a lot in the weeks since she'd visited. Several of the houses were enclosed, roofs were on most of them. Glaziers were working on two. But the office hadn't changed. Papers were still stacked in piles on both desks. Blueprints were pinned to the walls and on the drafting table. Yet there was a certain kind of order. Drea suspected Keith knew where everything was.

He was on the phone when she pushed opened the door. The cool air was a welcome relief. The day was hot and she seemed to be bothered more and more by the humid summer heat. The short walk from her car had seemed interminable.

"Hi. What brought you by?" he said when he hung up the phone.

"I brought you some lunch. I heard from the Realtor this morning. My tenants will be moving out by the end of the week. They found a nice house in Larchmont and can move right away."

She opened the bag and withdrew the thick roast beef sandwiches and chips.

"I was hoping you'd have something cold to drink."

"Sodas are in the small refrigerator over there," he said.

He reached for one of the sandwiches. Opening the bag

of chips, he shook some onto the paper plate.

"So you'll be ready to move back home then," he said.

Drea spun around, two cold sodas in her hand. She closed the refrigerator door with her hip, an odd pain piercing her heart at his comment.

"I guess I thought we'd both be moving into the house," she said carefully as she handed him a cold drink.

He raised his head to study her, his expression intent.

After a long moment he said slowly, "I don't know."

She fought the panic that threatened.

"You might as well move in until your folks get ready for their cruise. They'd probably like some time alone and there's time enough once they're gone to make up your mind. You'd be able to move back to their place while they were gone if you wanted to."

He nodded, slowly chewing his sandwich, his eyes never leaving hers. Drea lowered her gaze, picked up a sandwich, wondering if she'd be able to eat any of it. She was feeling slightly sick.

What else could she say to make him decide to move in with her? She didn't want him to end their marriage. Not yet. Not ever.

"All right. We'll move at the end of the month. Take it from there," he agreed.

Her hand trembled as she raised a chip to her mouth. She was afraid to meet his gaze, for fear he'd see the relief in hers. She still felt shaky and knew nothing had been resolved. But just as possession was nine-tenths of the law, so was proximity to love. Maybe he'd grow so used to having her around, he wouldn't want to change things.

"I'll arrange to have the furniture returned from storage. I thought of making the downstairs bedroom into an office. It's big enough for two desks—do you want me to get one for you?"

"Sure. I could do some of this paperwork at home if I had a place for it. Don't go spending much money, though."

She shook her head. "I won't."

His warning was clear–don't spend a lot on something that might not last beyond a few weeks.

Still, he could always take it with him if he left.

"What are you doing this afternoon?" he asked, finishing the last of his lunch.

She shrugged. "I'm taking your mom to the grocery store later, while your dad naps."

"It's one thing," he began conversationally, "to try to make it through the day without you when I have plenty of work to do and few reminders of you."

He stood right before her, his hands on her shoulders, drawing her closer and closer. "But it's quite another thing when you come calling." He kissed her.

"If I'm interrupting your work, I could leave," she said softly.

"No, I'm glad for the break."

Gathering up the remains of lunch, she glanced to make sure she hadn't missed anything. .

"I'll see you when you get home."

She turned for the door.

"Drea?"

Looking back, Drea waited.

"Did you mention to Mom or Dad that we might be moving at the end of the month?"

"No, I wanted to talk with you first."

"Hold off a day or so, will you? We'll tell them together, later."

"Are you having second thoughts?"

He shook his head. "No. I just want to wait a couple of days, all right?"

She nodded and let herself out of the office.

The heat and sun hit her the instant she closed the door behind her. But she didn't even notice the discomfort—she was too busy trying to understand why he'd want to wait to tell his parents they were moving out.

Chapter Seventeen

The next afternoon Drea stopped working on her book early and drove over to visit with Becky.

"This heat is wearing me out," Becky complained when they sat in the cool family room, large glasses of iced tea on the table before them.

"Me, too. I keep hoping for a series of thunderstorms to cool things down," Drea replied, leaning wearily against the sofa cushions. "For you, I'm sure it's worse—you have that baby in you to add to the discomfort."

"I know. Thank goodness it's only for another few weeks. Next time I'm going to plan to have the baby in the dead of winter!"

"Is there going to be a next time? Three kids is a bunch."

"I know, but Tom and I both love children. We're so happy doing things with Trevor and Tyler. If this one's another boy, I think we'll try one more time for a girl."

"And if it's a girl?"

"I don't know. I'd still like to have another one. We'll just have to see. So why aren't you and Keith starting a family?"

"Oh, you know. First we were in a foreign country. Now he wants to get the business going and all…"

Drea trailed off, wondering if what she suspected would change all that. She needed to find out, if only for her own sake.

"Do you mind that your dad gave Keith the family business?" she asked Becky.

"Not at all. He divided it up into shares and I'll get some income from it, as long as Keith keeps it going. I never was interested in it. If I hadn't married Tom, I was going to be a nurse, remember?"

"Yes. Do you regret giving that up?"

"Not a bit. I love my family, love spending my time with the boys. And now that you're back, I'm complete. I missed you this past year. Is marriage with my brother all you thought it would be?"

"Of course, why wouldn't it be?"

Drea was guarded in her reply. Did Becky suspect things weren't perfect?

"I just wondered. You've loved him for so long, I wondered if the reality would match the dream."

"It's different," Drea said.

Becky laughed and leaned over to squeeze her friend's hand.

"I bet. Anyway, you're good for him. He deserves to have someone adore him and you certainly have adored him forever."

"Is it so obvious?"

"Are you kidding? You hid it for years. If we hadn't been best friends, I'd never have suspected. Even now you don't seem to fully relax around him. But he does know, doesn't he?"

"What husband doesn't know how his wife feels?" Drea asked, then changed the subject.

She didn't want to go into all the details of her marriage, much as she longed to share the uncertainty and doubts she had.

She was married to Keith and owed him her first loyalty, even before her best friend.

But she wondered briefly if telling him she loved him would make any difference. She'd been so careful to keep her feelings hidden. Was that a mistake? Should she have told him from the beginning?

Drea tried to deny the envy she felt for her friend. Becky was so fortunate. She met Tom in college and they'd both known immediately that they were right for each other. Marrying before Becky graduated, they'd wasted no time in beginning their family. Soon their third child would be born into the love that surrounded each of their children.

Drea sighed and pulled into the driveway of the Branson's home. She cut the engine and leaned back. She was so tired she didn't even know if she could make it as far as the house.

With the air conditioner off, the Virginia heat began to seep into the car. Wearily she pushed open the door and headed for her room. She'd lie down, count her blessings and try to stamp out the envy that plagued her.

Why, she wondered as she sank gratefully back on the big queen-size bed, couldn't she and Keith have the same kind of love that Becky and Tom shared? These past three weeks had been blissfully happy ones for her. While she felt as if she were tiptoeing around on eggshells, she'd still enjoyed a closer relationship to Keith than ever before.

Slowly her hand came to her stomach. If what she was beginning to suspect was true, how would that change things? He'd make a wonderful father. Would he want to remain a husband, though?

She reached out for her pad. Darn, she'd left it down by her computer. She was too tired to get it. Nodding off to sleep, she made a mental note to add pregnancy test to her list of things to remember.

When Keith came home he was surprised to find Drea sound asleep in their bed. He hesitated in the doorway. She'd never taken a nap that he'd known about in the year they'd been married. Was she coming down with something?

"Drea?"

He crossed the room to the edge of the bed, sitting beside her.

"Umm?"

Slowly she opened her eyes, gazed at him for the longest moment without saying a word. Was she still sleeping, dreaming?

"Are you all right?" he asked.

She turned to look at the clock, her eyes widening in surprise at the lateness of the hour.

"Oh, gosh, I didn't mean to sleep for so long."

Sitting up, she ran her fingers through her hair and shook her head as if to clear the traces of sleep that clung.

"How come you needed a nap?"

He gently brushed her hair back from her face, letting the

soft tangles entrap his fingers.

"I was so tired. This heat's really getting to me."

She liked the feel of his fingers combing through her hair. "You've lived here all your life."

"I know. Maybe it's the humidity after the dry air in Kuwait. I'll be fine. Just needed a nap."

Keith waited, but she never met his eyes. Frowning in concern, he rose.

"I need to shower. Are you sure everything's all right?"

"Why wouldn't it be?" she asked.

He watched her for another moment, then turned to get clean clothes to take in the bathroom with him.

"I'm fine, really. I'll go help your mom with dinner," she said firmly.

Once he left the room, Drea groaned and fell back against the pillows. She was still tired! She wanted to just roll over and go back to sleep and not wake up until morning.

But she knew that'd worry everyone. And there may be no reason for it except the energy-zapping heat.

Slowly she rose. She wished she could splash some cold water on her face—maybe that'd help. Brushing her hair, she pinched her cheeks to get some color and headed down toward the kitchen. There were only a few hours to get through before she could go back to sleep.

Detouring through the dining room, she picked up her pad and added a reminder about the pregnancy test. Not that she thought she'd have trouble remembering that, but habits were hard to break. She tossed the pad onto the table and headed toward the kitchen. Hearing a plop, she turned. The pad had slid off the table onto the carpet. She stared at it.

She was so tired she couldn't even think. Measuring the distance from the door to the far side of the table, she shook her head and turned back to the kitchen. She'd pick it up later; right now she needed something to help her wake up.

Maybe iced tea would help or even iced coffee. Actually, bed was the only thing that would help.

Dinner was a strain. Keith watched her like a hawk. She drank several glasses of iced tea, but there was no punch from the caffeine. She still wanted to go back to sleep. She had trouble following the conversation and a couple of times was asked by Peggy or Matt if she was feeling all right.

When the dishes were done, Drea turned toward the backyard. They'd taken to sitting outside in the evenings, enjoying the cooler air after the heat of the day. She'd always been very fond of Becky's parents, but now she was getting to know them even better and loved them both.

"Dear, why don't you go on up to bed? You might be coming down with something and maybe a good night's sleep would nip it in the bud," Peggy suggested, coming up and putting her arm around Drea's shoulders.

"That does sound good," Drea said wistfully, watching Keith and his father laughing at some joke.

"Go on. We'll see you in the morning."

"I don't want Keith to worry."

"I'll tell him you're fine. Go on."

Drea nodded grateful for Peggy's understanding. She walked through the dining room and picked up her pad. She knew she was exhausted when the effort to do so was almost more than she could stand. Carrying it upstairs, she put it on the dresser. Rummaging in the drawer, she found the sexy nightie she'd bought. For some reason she wanted to wear the nightgown tonight.

In less than ten minutes she was in bed. In less than one minute after that she was sound asleep.

Keith had left for work by the time Drea awoke the next morning. She felt much better, refreshed and full of energy. Thank goodness all she'd needed was a good night's sleep.

Plot ideas and characterization traits were bubbling around in her mind as she sat down to her computer. The rest had definitely helped her creativity. The morning flew by as she typed page after page.

Drea stretched and decided to take a break surprised to discover it was already lunchtime. She'd grab a bite to eat and make her trip to the drugstore before Peggy and Matt needed to leave for the weekly visit to his doctor.

Nervous energy tingled inside. What would Keith say if she was pregnant? Would he be happy about it?

They'd never discussed children since the marriage wasn't supposed to last beyond the tour in Kuwait.

He'd questioned her that first night they made love. She'd honestly thought she was safe. He'd been so careful to use a condom every other time.

Shy about the entire situation, Drea drove to a neighborhood where she didn't normally shop. She wasn't going to give rise to any gossip. If the test proved positive, she'd tell Keith first.

By the time she returned home dark clouds were building on the horizon. Wind rustled the leaves on the trees. The signs of an impending thunderstorm were everywhere. She hurried into the house.

"I'm not late, am I?" she asked as Peggy and Matt met her at the door.

"No. We thought we'd allow a bit extra time to drive. If it starts raining, we didn't want to feel rushed. I've left the windows open," Peggy said.

Drea nodded. "I'll leave them that way until it actually begins to rain. Drive carefully."

The wind that blew the curtains into billowing clouds away from the windows would cool the house and refresh the air. Time enough to shut windows when the rain started.

Her cell phone rang. It was her agent. Drea listened, blinking in shock. Slowly she took a deep breath.

"Repeat that, Jack."

When he complied, she let out a shriek and twirled around and around, getting dizzy in her excitement.

"You did it! You pulled it off! I don't believe it," she shouted into the receiver.

A major television network was opting on an agreement to use her books as the basis for a new TV series. Her approval on scripts and casting was included. It was the deal of a lifetime and Jack had pulled it off!

"What? Yes, yes, email me a copy of the letter of intent. I want to read every single word. Oh, my goodness, Jack, I can't believe it!"

After she finished the exciting call, she fairly flew across the room to her computer, impatiently waiting until Jack's email showed up in her inbox. She eagerly read every single word.

Wait until she told Keith!

Wait until Becky heard, she'd go bananas!

She looked at her cell phone. No, she didn't want to tell Keith that way. She'd wait until he came home. And she had to tell him first. This was about the most exciting thing that had ever happened to her. She was delirious with happiness.

She printed out a copy of the letter and reread it. She jotted a couple of questions in the margin to talk to Jack about. Mostly she was giddy with excitement!

She took it upstairs to put it with her other writing correspondence. She kept all her records in one box—her royalty statements, contracts, agreement with her agent, all the papers related to her writing. Not very businesslike, but it suited her. Proudly she placed the latest letter on top.

She still had the small brown bag she'd brought up earlier. Drawing out the pregnancy test kit, she opened it and read the instructions. She'd have to wait until morning. Which was too bad, she had the house to herself right now.

The wait would seem endless, but she didn't mind, not with the other news bubbling to be shared. Replacing the kit in the bag, she put it beneath the sink.

The wind was blowing harder than ever. Drea went to the window and looked out across the backyard. The tree limbs moved in a swirling dance as their leaves fluttered beneath the unceasing breeze. She relished the coolness of the air. The thunderstorm would bring down the temperature. She, for one, would be glad of it.

Turning, she headed back downstairs to her computer, wondering if she'd be able to write anything when she felt too excited to even think?

Chapter Eighteen

Keith pulled the truck to a stop. The car was gone. It was the middle of the afternoon. He thought his father had a doctor's appointment today. He glanced again at the dark sky. The storm would hit in minutes. He'd let everybody go home early. There'd be no working in a building site during a thunderstorm–it was too dangerous.

And, he hesitated to admit it even to himself, he was anxious to see Drea. He'd been worried about her last night.

She'd still been sleeping when he left this morning. He hoped she wasn't getting sick.

When he walked into the kitchen, he could hear the click of her computer keys. Moving quietly to the connecting door, he watched her work. Her concentration was devoted to the screen before her as her fingers flew across the keyboard.

Quietly he backed away and headed upstairs. He'd shower first, then let her know he was home.

The wind was blowing hard. The door to their room had been propped open, to keep it from slamming shut with the force of the wind. It felt good. It was time for the heat to break. Once the rain ended, everything would be fresh and clean and the air much cooler.

He drew out clean jeans, a shirt. The wind fluttered the pages of a pad, flipping them open, sliding the pad across the dresser.

Smiling, Keith reached out and smoothed down the pages. It was Drea's notepad. She was always making lists. He picked it up. He'd place it—

His eyes caught the words and he paused, reading.

He felt as if he'd been kicked in the gut.

He dropped the clean clothes on the bed, sank down on the edge as he read the list.

"Get sexy nightie…Verify joint checking…Make Keith's favorite meals…Mercedes vs. Maserati…Check insurance/inheritance…Pregnancy test."

Pregnancy test? His hand gripped the pad so tightly the cardboard bent.

He been played.

She was exactly like Diane. Deceitful. Duplicite. He should have suspected.

They'd a distant relationship in Kuwait. When they returned home, when there was a distinct possibility his father wouldn't make it, suddenly Drea changed.

She began flirting, trying to make him jealous with her talk of dating other men. Doing all in her power to ensnare him with concern about his father until he'd actually entertained thoughts about making their marriage permanent.

But she'd never said she loved him. It had all been a carefully staged plan. She'd even written everything down!

Rising, he went into the bathroom and looked at the counter. Nothing. Opening the medicine cabinet, he saw nothing out of the ordinary. He opened the cupboard beneath the sink. Drawing out the brown bag, he took out the pregnancy kit.

If she thought she'd trap him into continuing this mockery of a marriage by getting pregnant, it was time she found out he wasn't going to play that game.

He took a deep breath. The rage that was building was like nothing he'd ever experienced. Even Diane's betrayal hadn't caused such anger.

His father was recovered enough to stand the knowledge that Keith and Drea were no longer a couple.

Her house was vacant—she could move back today. He'd help her. He wanted her gone so he never had to see her again.

Slowly he turned and headed downstairs. He crossed to his father's office. Unused since his heart attack, it was empty. Keith placed the kit and the pad in the center of the desk, pushing aside some folders.

He took a deep breath which didn't help at all. He clenched his fists.

He refused to hurt her, though he longed to smash something his anger ran so deep.

He refused to rant and rage like he wanted to.

He'd call her in, demand an explanation about what he'd found and then get her out of his life.

Deep inside, beneath the hot anger that threatened to swamp him, was a profound hurt. He'd begun to trust her. Now this. He didn't know how he'd live the rest of his life knowing what she'd done.

But he would.

He went to the dining room.

"Drea, could I see you a moment?"

"Keith? Hi."

Her smile was wide and open. Almost like the ones she gave to Becky. "I didn't know you were home…" she trailed off when she realized he wasn't smiling in return.

"In my father's office."

He didn't know where his folks were, but he didn't want them barging in on this confrontation.

"Sure. Is something wrong?"

Drea got up and followed him into the office.

Keith closed the door, watching her. He saw her start when she saw the pregnancy test kit on the desk. And the pad. Had she thought he wouldn't ever discover her treachery?

"Oh," she said.

"Is that all you have to say? Oh?"

He moved to the open window, hoping the breeze would cool him enough to deal with her rationally, calmly. He wanted to put his fist through something.

"I was going to tell you if the results were positive."

"Nice of you."

"You don't want a baby, I take it." Her voice sounded strained.

He swung around.

"Did you think to trap me that way? You should have checked first."

"Trap you? What are you talking about?"

"Your great plan to trap me into the kind of marriage you wanted. Nice try, but no thanks."

"I don't know what you're talking about."

He crossed to the desk and picked up the notepad.

"Let me read you some of your checklist for entrapment. Get sexy clothes, make favorite meals, joint bank account, pregnancy. You have check marks by some of these, but not all. You still haven't decided whether you want a Mercedes or a Maserati. You still don't know the inheritance situation or the insurance."

He tossed the pad back and glared at her.

"And there's no need for you to know. This marriage is finished. I'm exercising my rights in the prenuptial agreement and ending it now. According to the agreement you signed a year ago, you get nothing. So all your efforts have blown up in your face."

He wanted to shake her until she begged his forgiveness. He wanted to take her upstairs and make love to her until she promised that she wanted only him and not his money or the things his money could buy.

She was staring at him as if he'd grown a second head.

"You're nuts. You are absolutely, certifiably nuts. That list is for my book."

"Fix Keith's favorite dinners is for your book?" he said in total disbelief.

"No. Some of it's personal. I need to jot things down to remember them. It's a habit. You know that."

"I know that for all the months we were in Kuwait you couldn't be bothered treating me any differently from the way you had the past few years. But the moment we arrived in Virginia, the moment you realized what a gold mine I'd have if something happened to my father, everything changed. You saw me as a meal ticket for life and did all you could to latch on to that with both hands."

"That's not true," she whispered, looking horrified.

"Of course it is, admit it. What about those sexy clothes you recently bought and wore with the intent of enticing me? It was just as hot in Kuwait, but you didn't buy new clothes there."

"Hardly. I was trying to behave with circumspection in an Arab country. It's hot here and not unusual to wear clothes suitable for the heat."

"Ah, but you seem to have forgotten I already went through this once. I know the drill. And I protected myself against you."

When she backed up against the door, his temper flared. Turning, he crossed to the window.

"You can pack your bags and move out today. I'll make your excuses to my folks."

"Keith, listen to me. That list is about my story. Some of it was about you, but most of it's about my story."

He ignored her. Counting the seconds until she'd leave.

He pulled back when he he heard sob.

She was crying.

He looked at her standing by the door. She glared at him as the tears traced their way down her cheeks. But her chin was tilted and she didn't move.

"You have me confused with Diane. I did not marry you for your money. I have never asked you for anything beyond the household expenses, which you said you wanted to provide. You arrogant jerk. You think money's so important?"

"It is to those who don't have it. Weren't you the one who told me all your father's insurance money had to go to his last illness? The income from Branson Construction must have looked mighty fine to you."

"Oh, you idiot. I've loved you since I was sixteen years old and I don't have a clue why. You laughed at me when I was a teenager. I stayed away after that because I couldn't bear it. I couldn't come to your wedding when you married someone else. I thought the happiest day of my life was the one when you asked me to marry you. But you're so warped by what happened with Diane that you can't see someone who loves you when they stand right in front of you. I'd have done anything for you and this is the way you treat me."

"Love, ha! Where was this great love while we were in Kuwait? Why am I only hearing about it now, when I've discovered your deception? We've been sharing the same bed for weeks, never a peep about love from you all this time. We've been making love and never a peep. How much is this love worth—half my inheritance?"

He glared at her.

She glared back.

Taking a deep breath, she said, "Wait right here, you self-righteous pig. Don't you move a muscle. I'll be right back!"

She spun around and disappeared up the stairs.

Keith was breathing hard. He clenched his fists and glared at the furniture in the study. Moving to sit in the chair behind the desk, he glanced at the note pad. He snatched it up and flung it across the room. He wished he'd never found the blasted thing. He wished he was still living in some fairy-tale existence where he could wonder if marriage was in his future. If sharing his life with Drea were a possibility.

He stared at the pregnancy kit, his thoughts spinning so fast he couldn't analyze how he felt.

A baby. Were they really going to have a baby?

Could he end things if there was a baby?

Who would take care of Drea? Or the baby?

The door slammed shut behind her. He looked up, struck with how beautiful she looked, even as furious as she definitely was. She had a bunch of papers in her hand and fiery anger in her eyes. Locking her gaze to his, she crossed the room to stand before the desk.

"You've ruined what could have been a wonderful day for me. You've probably ruined both our lives with your unfounded accusations and your inability to trust someone who loves you more than anything. You needn't worry about me anymore, Keith Branson. I'll be gone before you know it. You didn't want me to love you when I was sixteen and it's obvious you don't want my love now. So be it."

"Drea-"

"Shut up. I'm the one talking now. You had your say."

She thumbed through the papers and withdrew one, slamming it down on the desk. "Here is my first contract. Please note the advance."

Another paper followed.

"Here's my latest royalty statement. Please note the amount. I think it's fairly obvious I could buy anything I want."

Two more papers were slammed down before him. He

couldn't even read the first one—she wasn't giving him a moment.

"Here are contracts two and three. Check out the escalation clauses."

She paused for breath, her gaze never returning to his, even though he gave up looking at the papers she kept slapping down on his desk and kept his eyes on her.

He wanted to kiss her again. He really didn't want to hurt her, except to retaliate for her actions, her betrayal.

For a moment he felt the prick of tears. Clenching his jaw, he looked up from her mouth. He hadn't cried since he was a boy—he sure wasn't going to now.

"—going to tell you tonight. I thought you'd be so happy for me. Shows what a lousy judge of character I am."

He blinked, glanced at the latest document she threw down. "What is it?"

"The result of weeks of negotiations. My book is going to be the basis for a weekly TV series. Trust me, Keith, your money is the last thing in this world I need. I'll make so much off this I won't be able to spend it all in my lifetime. So take your precious construction company and all the money you make from it and enjoy it in your old age. The baby and I don't need you."

Tears were running down her cheeks, but she still glared at him. Snatching up the pregnancy test kit, she stormed out of the room, slamming the door behind her again.

Keith felt as if a whirlwind had swept through. He glanced down at the letter on top of the pile of papers she'd delivered. Reading it through, he shook his head. She was going to make a fortune with this deal. Slowly he picked up the next one and read it.

Read them all.

Rain started falling and he got up to shut the window, all but an inch or two. He still needed the cooling air to cool his temper.

He continued reading, studied the royalty statements. She'd included her bank statement. While she couldn't buy and sell him today, she came close to it. All this time he thought he was supporting her and she had enough money after the first royalty check to live comfortably for a long, long time.

I've loved you since I was sixteen years old.

He leaned back in the chair. If it were true, he probably succeeded in his wish to hurt her as much as he was hurting.

He should have asked for an explanation, not jumped right in with accusations.

He should have known better.

He did know better.

He known her for years. He had lived with her for eleven months.

Drea was nothing like Diane or the others. He *knew* that.

How could he have thought otherwise for even a minute?

Slowly Keith rose, his anger gone. He'd apologize, explain why he'd thought what he'd thought.

She'd understand. She had to.

He opened the office door. The wind was blowing rain in through his mother's windows. Quickly he went around the ground floor, closing windows, wiping up the rain. He went upstairs. Their door was wide open. The rain blew in across the floor, reaching the bed. The window hadn't been closed. He slammed it shut and looked around.

Where was Drea? She hadn't been downstairs. He thought she was up here.

He looked across the hall. The bathroom door was open. For the second time that day he felt as if he'd been kicked. She was gone.

Chapter Nineteen

Where?

He looked out the window. It was pouring. Lightning flashed and a short time later the harsh crack of thunder shattered the afternoon.

He crossed to the guest room in the front of the house and looked out. The truck was still there. Where had she gone in this downpour?

He went back to the study and called his sister. A few minutes later, he hung up. Drea wasn't there, but Becky said she'd call him if she heard from Drea.

Staring out at the thunderstorm, he hoped she wasn't walking in it. Maybe she'd gone to one of the neighbors.

Truly worried now, he reached for the phone and began searching for his wife.

It was almost dark when Keith pulled into the driveway. Cutting the engine, he climbed out, carrying a small package. The storm had blown itself out, the air was fresh and clean.

The last of the stormy afternoon faded into darkness as the clouds dissipated. He heard the buzz of the crickets as they began their nightly song. The air had cooled, yet it was still warm.

Mounting the shallow steps to the wide porch, he wondered if she were here. He didn't know where else to look, he'd already tried every other place he could think of.

His expression wavered between frustration and determination, uncertainty and hope. The entire afternoon had been miserable. Had he lost everything?

Lost his wife, a family, a future worth having?

Reaching the front door, he peered through the glass oval into the dark, empty house. No lights anywhere. He didn't know where else to look.

He had to find her. He needed to talk to her, get his life back on track.

For a moment fear touched him. If he could get his life back on track.

Walking around to the back of the house, he spotted her. She was sitting on the big porch swing, alone, in the dark.

For a moment he remembered finding her like this a year ago after her dad had died.

The night he'd come to make his pitch.

Skirting one of the many islands of flowers in the green lawn, he approached her, waiting for her to notice him. He could smell the honeysuckle that clung to the back fence, the sweet scent adding to the reminiscences of that night a year ago.

She'd been sad then, too.

"Drea?"

She looked up.

"Keith? What are you doing here?"

In three strides he joined her on the swing, sank down beside her.

She'd been crying. He could see it on her face and in the damp tissues she clutched in her hand. Her dress was rumpled, her feet tucked up beneath the skirt.

For a second something twisted deep within him.

He'd caused this anguish.

He hoped he could end it.

"I had to find you," he said softly.

Without thinking about it, he reached out and drew her up against him, praying she wouldn't resist.

Drea held herself stiffly until, unable to resist, she gradually relaxed against him as his hand gently rubbed her back.

He said nothing.

She remained silent.

For over a decade he'd thought of her almost as a sister.

Once again he remembered the day he met her. He let himself remember the weeks that followed when she'd revealed the crush she had on him.

Only she'd called it love.

For eleven years, she'd called it love.

And as he had before, he'd once again thrown it back in her face.

"I'm sorry." His voice was low.

He wanted to say more, but the words wouldn't come. Slowly he brushed his fingers against her arm, feeling the satin heat beneath them.

She remained silent.

Had he ruined it? Had he been too slow in learning the truth to save his marriage–which he now knew he wanted more than anything in the world?

Why was it only when something was lost that its full value was realized?

He tried to think how to bring up the subject uppermost in his mind without sounding crass and insensitive. His heart pounded. There was no delaying.

"When will you use the pregnancy test?" he asked finally.

Drea shrugged. "In the morning. Don't worry, I won't be a burden."

He closed his eyes at her words, the pain piercing his heart.

"You've never been a burden. I never thought you'd be."

She stirred and pulled away. He pushed them back and forth on the swing, frustration sizzling as she rejected his touch.

"Drea, I have an idea I want you to seriously consider," he began hesitantly.

He needed her to say yes. He needed to present it properly, to make sure he gave her no reason to refuse.

She had to listen to him!

"Not this time, Keith. You had an idea last year and look where it got me. I should have refused you then. I, too, have learned something over the last year."

He closed his eyes, then snapped them open. The sky was black, the stars scattered across like brilliant diamonds.

He sighed. It wouldn't be easy.

But he'd had a lot of time to think after she'd left this afternoon. Now he had to make things right.

If he ever wanted a moment of peace and happiness, he had to make things right.

"I'm not very good at this," he said.

"Go home, Keith. There's nothing left to talk about. You were very clear in your opinion and feelings this afternoon."

"No. I have to say a few things. Then I'll leave."

He hoped he wouldn't be leaving, but that was up to Drea.

"What?"

He took a deep breath. Her tone didn't sound very promising, but then he couldn't blame her after all he'd said that afternoon.

"We met when you were sixteen and I was twenty."

She crossed her arms and stared out over the gray yard.

"So you didn't know me in high school," he continued.

"If we're here to rehash old days—"

"Hear me out, Drea, that's all I want."

Not everything he wanted by a long shot, but all he felt he had a right to for the time being.

"When I was a junior I made quarterback on the football team. That same fall I met Sara Carter. She was the prettiest thing I'd seen up to that point. We started dating and soon were going steady. Late in the fall of my senior year I pulled a shoulder muscle pretty badly. It looked as if I wouldn't be able to play in any more games. That's when Sara discovered she really didn't love me. She was attracted to the quarterback who could still play ball and garner the adulation of the other students."

Keith was watching Drea. He saw her turn to look at him.

"You know about Diane, now you know about Sara. There was a girl in college, too, who wanted what I had to offer more than she wanted me." He shook his head. "Do you wonder with my track record that I'm not more trusting around women? Even around women who I know are different?"

"I guess not," she said softly.

"Here, this is for you."

He thrust the wrapped present into her lap. "I was kind of hoping you'd wear it whenever I get bent out of shape and start throwing accusations."

He hoped she'd be around when he got bent out of shape the next time. He hoped he hadn't ruined their lives, as she'd said earlier.

Drea lifted the package, slid a finger beneath the taped end and ripped the paper. She withdrew a T-shirt. Holding it up, she could tell it had something on the front.

"A shirt?" she asked.

"Yes. I had it specially made."

"It's too dark to see it."

He pulled out his cell phone and turned on the flashlight app, pointing it at the shirt.

"It says I am not Diane, emphasis on the not."

Drea crushed the shirt to her, closing her eyes against the surge of emotions that swept through her.

Why was he here? What did he really want?

Dare she let herself hope he'd changed his mind?

She looked at him as he clicked off the light, wishing she

could know what he was thinking.

She cleared her throat. "So I'm to wear this—"

"The next time I behave like a total idiot. I don't want to end our marriage. I want to be with you tomorrow when you take that pregnancy test. If you're pregnant, I want to know as soon as you do. Honey baby, I want you like I've never wanted anyone else. I'm sorry for my temper this afternoon, sorry for the harsh things I said. Don't leave, stay with me and make our marriage work."

Time stood still. The star-sprinkled sky gave no answer when she searched it. Drea didn't know what to say. She longed to agree to stay with him, but doubt and hurt made her hesitate. What about the next time something set him off?

She smiled slowly. She could always wear the T-shirt.

"Drea?"

"I don't know, Keith," she began.

He exhaled as if he'd been holding his breath and reached out to draw her into his lap, settling her against his chest, his arms locked firmly around her.

"Tell me you don't love me anymore. Tell me you lied about loving me since you were sixteen and I'll get up and leave. I won't contest any divorce and if you're pregnant, I'll set up a trust for our baby. But if you can't tell me all that, then I'm not going anywhere."

Stalling for time, hoping she'd think up the right thing to say, she traced her fingers across his shoulder, liking the strength she felt beneath the cotton, longing to touch his bare skin, to have him touch her.

"I thought you only wanted a temporary marriage."

"A year ago that's what I thought, too. Now I want forever."

"Why?"

She felt cherished being held in his arms. Her head rested on his shoulder and she closed her eyes as he spoke. She'd always loved his voice. As much as she loved every other aspect of Keith Branson.

"Did you know I was secretly flattered that you had that crush on me when we first met?" he asked.

"Right. You showed me how you felt."

Even now, a decade later, she felt the sting of rejection at his mocking laughter.

"No, I showed you how an arrogant man child shows off to his peer group, too afraid to let his real feelings show, lest he be the butt of ridicule. I was flattered. If you hadn't suddenly started acting like I was poison, I might have asked you out."

"I overheard you and some of your friends laughing at me. Of course I stayed away," she said slowly.

"Honey baby, I'm sorry." He rested his cheek on her hair.

The blood roared through her veins, her heart pounded. She couldn't hide her feelings around this man. She'd loved him as long as she'd known him—nothing had changed.

All the anger and harsh words in the world wouldn't change her.

"You don't need to be tied to me. And if I'm pregnant, you can still see our baby."

He tipped up her chin. Drea caught the gleam in his eyes as he rubbed a thumb over her lips.

"I love you, Drea. I realized that today. That was part of

the reason I was so angry. I felt more betrayed than I ever felt with Diane. I thought a part of me had been ripped out and trampled. When you left, when I couldn't find you, I knew then what my life would be like if our marriage ended. I can't imagine living until Christmas without you, much less the rest of my life. Say you'll forgive me for my temper today. Tell me you love me enough to give me another chance. I'll cherish you until I die. Don't let today's mistake keep us apart."

"Oh, Keith, I love you so much I ache with it."

She wanted to tell him how much he'd always meant to her, but his mouth covered hers and she was lost.

He trailed kisses down her throat, sipping at the sweet nectar as he traced her collarbone, dipped even lower. Drea gave herself up to joy only Keith brought, her heart swelling with happiness.

He raised his head as she gazed up at him.

"There's probably not a bed in the house," he grumbled.

She shook her head. "No, but there's plenty of grass. A high hedge for privacy and fireflies to light the night."

She wanted to be closer, so close they were one. She was on fire for him, desperate to show how much she loved him.

"It's wet."

"So what? Come on."

Drea stood up and pulled him up with her. In three steps they were in the thick grass beside the house.

"You are so beautiful," Keith said.

"Hurry," she urged him.

He held off. "You never said if we're staying married."

Drea laughed. "You had to ask? Yes and yes and yes. For

a smart man, you are an idiot sometimes."

Epilogue

"Drea?"

"I'm upstairs," she called back, rocking the baby gently. He was almost asleep. His tummy full, he was no longer sucking. In a moment he'd drop off and she'd put him to bed.

"What—Oh, is he sleeping?"

Keith came quietly into the bright, cheerful nursery.

"Almost. What did you need?"

He grinned and leaned over to kiss her softly.

"I need you."

He kissed her again, his fingertips trailing down across her exposed breast.

"You're still the prettiest thing I ever saw."

"I thought that was Sara What's-her-name," Drea said against his mouth, leaning forward for another kiss.

He stood up and gently took the now-sleeping baby from her.

"That was in high school. My standards have risen since then. You now rank as the prettiest thing I've ever seen. Especially when holding Matthew."

Drea smiled at the compliment. The past year had been

wonderful. She knew she'd never been happier.

"What did you want?"

She joined Keith as he laid the baby in the crib, covering him lightly. Matthew was growing so fast he'd soon be able to sit up by himself. Then he'd be walking and who knew what kind of mischief he'd get into?

"Did the mail come?" she asked, leaning against him as she watched their son settle down.

"Yes, and you got a ton of stuff. There's an envelope from your agent. Looks like maybe line edits on the latest book. Then there's a packet from the studio. Do you have more scripts to approve?"

"I don't know. I thought I was caught up. I'll have to see. Is that why you called me?"

Keith put his arm around her shoulder and walked her from the nursery. Turning down the hall to their room, he didn't stop until they were inside.

"Actually, I came to ask you something, but now that I know Matthew's asleep and we have a few hours before we go to dinner at Becky's, I've thought of something better to do."

"Better than what?"

She smiled as he drew his shirt over his head and threw it across the room. The familiar tug of excitement and anticipation began to build. She still hadn't outgrown the shimmering waves of awareness that flooded her body any time she was near this sexy man.

She began to unbutton her top.

"Better than working on the mower. Which is why I called you. I found the T-shirt I bought you in the rag pile."

She nodded, "I don't need it anymore," she said, drawing back the spread.

He picked her up and spun them both around twice before falling back on the mattress, still holding her in his arms. "Why is that?"

He kissed her.

When she could speak again, Drea snuggled up against her husband.

"The reason I no longer need that T-shirt is that I am totally convinced that you love me. I don't want any reminders of the past—it's gone and forgotten. I only want the shining future that you offer me."

"Ah, honey baby, I love you."

—The End—

More books by Barbara McMahon

The Talmadge Sisters
Letters to Caroline
Michelle's Marriage Deal
Trusting Abby

The Harts of Texas Series
Rebel Heart
Tangled Hearts
Reckless Heart

Cowboy Heroes Series
Blue Bells on the Hill
Cowboy's Bride
One Stubborn Cowboy
Crazy About a Cowboy
Never Doubt a Cowboy
Cowboy Marshal
Summer Cowboy
Second Chance Cowboy
Movie Star Cowboy

Tropical Escape Series
Island Rendezvous
Come into the Sun
Island Paradise
Destination Romance Boxed Set

Rocky Point Series
The Family Next Door
Rocky Point Reunion
Rocky Point Promise
Rocky Point Hero

Elite Security Mystery Series
Trusting Jake

The Ultimate Billionaires
The Cynical Sheikh
Falling for the Sheikh
A Sheikh of Her Own
The Unforgettable Sheikh

Other Books
A Soldier's Christmas
I'll Take Forever
Jared's Promise
The Paper Marriage
The Christmas Locket
The Banished Bride
Cowboy Charade
The Cowboy's Special Christmas
Mail Order Bride
Because of You